Sudden violent death awaits...

Emily Cross, the small-town girl from Iowa, held the cigarette to her red lips, drawing in a deep drag. Her head was slightly cocked to one side. She sat on the couch facing the front window. The acrid smoke curled from between her lips as she released it from her lungs. Her eyes were closed.

One bare leg was folded underneath her cutoffs, and the purple tube top she wore strained to hold her full breasts. She was proud of her girls and considered them her best asset. Men usually agreed with her.

Bruce seemed like a nice guy. She liked him, but then again, like Sharon, she liked most men. She wondered why Sharon had taken up with that loser Rocky Wilson, though. He was a slob, a drunk, and not too bright.

Maybe she'd wanted to get control of that hair shop. Sharon had often said she wanted to own her own shop one day. Emily smirked. Sharon had said a lot of things.

Maybe I should give Bruce the tapes Sharon made of her phone calls? He might be able to use them, they are his now anyway. She wasn't about to give them to those creepy cops.

Those damn cops had been very nosy about her roomie when they'd ransacked the house. They'd said she was missing and maybe dead or something. Emily had almost laughed aloud at that. Sharon was always off on one of her adventures. Many a time she'd disappeared for days, shacking up with some guy and then coming home looking like she'd been ridden hard then thrown out with the trash.

Emily's ears perked up when she heard the squeak of brakes being applied and the sound of a throaty engine dying off in the driveway. Opening her eyes, she stood up and walked to the door.

The coal-black sky and cool wind made her shiver. It was late afternoon and it would be night soon. She couldn't make out who was in the blue truck parked outside. She had seen the truck before and knew it wasn't Rocky's. That scumbag had hit on her more than once, but he was too old and creepy for her tastes.

She padded back to the couch on her bare feet and sat down again to wait for the doorbell. There was a knock, accompanied by the sound of breaking glass. The exterior light on the landing went out.

She stood, shrugged, and then walked to the door, still holding the lit cigarette, its trail of white smoke following her. Flinging open the door, she intended to raise some serious shit over the light bulb. Those damn things were expensive.

Her anger turned to fear when a figure dressed in a black leather jacket, black gloves, and a black balaclava appeared in front of her.

A scream caught in her throat when she spotted the long-bladed knife in the right hand of the strange figure. The knife flashed toward her. Instantly, blinding pain shot across her neck. Dropping the cigarette, her hands went to her throat. Something warm and sticky flowed over her fingers. Her knees became weak and she struggled to remain upright, leaning against the door frame.

Her vision clouded and she shivered. It's so cold....

Her final thought before the darkness enveloped her was, why?

SHEAR MURDER

A Trudy Wilson Mystery

RUSS CROSSLEY

53RD STREET PUBLISHING

Other titles in the Trudy Wilson Mystery series

Shear Murder

Bad Loyalty

Buzzcut (coming in the fall of 2015)

Dedication

This book is dedicated to my biggest fan, Rita, my wife of more than 30 years and my great love. Thanks, darling, for your love and support.

Acknowledgment

Many thanks to my editor, Colleen Kuehne, for her excellent editorial assistance with this series. Without her expertise this book would never have been what it is.

SHEAR MURDER

Russ Crossley

53rd Street Publishing

1st edition Copyright © 2012 Russ Crossley
2nd edition revised Copyright © 2014 Russ Crossley

Trade paperback ISBN 978-1-927621-34-9
Ebook ISBN 978-1-927621-11-0
Cover image © Fabian Schmidt | Dreamstime.com

Published by:
53rd Street Publishing
Gibsons B.C. Canada
www.53rdsteetpublishing.com

Prologue

SHARON RAN. Her mouth dry from gulping air. Her heart pounded in her chest. Her shoulder length blonde hair hung limply around her oval shaped face rain soaked strands slapping her skin.

The wet sand was cool between her toes. To her right, the surf appeared from the darkness, a wall of seething foam. It slammed into the sand a few feet in front of her, sending a wall of air pressure against her skin and causing her to stumble. But she quickly regained her footing. She'd lost her shoes father back, but that didn't matter to her. Survival was all that mattered now.

In her rising panic and the darkness, she wasn't sure anymore if she was following the curve of the beach or was headed toward the pounding surf. In the last few minutes, the glowing moon had disappeared behind the dark, angry clouds and now stinging drops of rain blinded her. She frantically tried to blink the cold water away, but it did no good; the rain was coming faster, harder now.

The sand made her slip and slide as she ran. She could hear the panting of her pursuer, closing from behind. She willed her tired legs to move faster. Faster than she'd ever been able to run before in her life. Her heart raced in her chest and fear kept her going.

The panting behind her lessened. She hoped he'd given up. Slowing, she took a quick peek over her left shoulder. In the dim light, she saw him, bent over, holding his thighs. She had won.

She would live.

Her breath left her when she was slammed off her feet by thousands of cold needles and was lifted off the ground by dark, icy water. A numbing cold caught her voice and wouldn't let her scream. With her mouth full of salt water, she struggled to reach solid ground. Her chest ached as water filled her nose and mouth. Her eyes went wide with terror as she realized what was happening to her. I can't breath. I'm drowning.

A sneaker wave. It was to be her last thought as the dark, freezing water engulfed her and dragged her farther from the shore. The numbing cold of the ocean made her muscles seize up. Unable to move her arms or legs, Sharon Carstairs disappeared into the inky depths of the vast Pacific, in the embrace of a receding killer wave.

One

March, and the salty, icy wind blew hard across her face as she walked toward the locked glass door of the Hair Club beauty shop in the Bricktown Plaza. At least the metaphorical wolves from the bank had finally disappeared from the door. Sharon Carstaris had made that possible, not her own business acumen.

Trudy Wilson sighed as she brushed the stray strands of mouse-brown hair away from her face, then pulled her key ring from her jacket pocket. The burden of debt she'd been carrying was finally beginning to disappear from between her narrow shoulders.

The lights inside the shop were set on dim as she had instructed Sharon to leave them each night at closing time. The local cops patrolled the parking lot at night, and they liked to be able to see inside without getting out of their plain white cruisers—the ones with the row of red and blue lights atop a bar on the roof.

Trudy thought of Sharon Carstairs, with her pleasant smile and her flowing blonde curls. The golden cascade down her back made her look younger than her chronological age.

Sharon's girl-next-door attitude belied her true nature. Behind that innocence, Sharon held her secrets close, locked away from prying eyes.

Trudy had hired the 40-ish blonde some six months ago, and soon realized she didn't know much about Sharon. What Trudy did know was that her and her husband Rocky's cash reserves were nearing the end. Bankruptcy had been hounding their every waking moment for months and would have continued if it weren't for Sharon and her client list.

At first, Sharon seemed to be the answer to all her problems.

Sharon said she had worked for a few different shops in Newport over the past twenty years. She volunteered no specifics about her previous employers and Trudy didn't press her. Ignorance, at times, was a useful thing. The only thing Sharon did tell Trudy was that she had moved up the Oregon coast to get away from what she called "family problems."

Trudy, being new to the business world, felt she shouldn't pry, so she let it go without checking work or personal references and hired the pretty blonde.

The shop consisted of six chairs, with Trudy and Sharon working two of them. The other four were unused for the moment.

Trudy had moved to Fairview from Seattle five months ago, specifically to open her own hair shop. Prior to moving, Rocky had owned a small auto parts supply company, and had been reasonably successful. He had sold the business so they could enjoy the country lifestyle here on the Oregon coast. Unfortunately, he hadn't had a job since arriving and had become depressed and retreated into a bottle.

To compound her money troubles, small-town people take quite a time to accept new people moving into the area, and as a result, Trudy had had few customers.

The addition of the sunny, blonde-haired stylist, with her tight black leotards and loose fitting tee shirts, which did little to disguise her ample breasts, had made all the difference.

14

Sharon was a welcome sight to the men in town. Consequently, business began to increase at a steady pace shortly after she arrived.

Sharon was quickly building a clientele. Men would stop and talk, especially when she washed the windows or energetically swept the brick sidewalk. There was Mr. Keelson, the bakery shop owner with the fringe of gray around his mostly bald head, and Mr. Williams, the postman who stopped by on his route on Tuesdays. They were among the many admirers of the buxom blonde. Mr. Johnson liked his chestnut brown hair cut short. He'd been a client since the first time he came in and Sharon made him laugh.

At the supermarket, while elbow deep in the apple bin, Trudy overheard two women extolling the virtues of the new hairdresser from Newport at the Hair Club. She knew then she'd made the right decision.

Slipping the bronze key into the lock on the door, Trudy turned it and heard the familiar click as the bolt disengaged. Pulling on the aluminum handle, she entered the shop. The air inside wasn't really warm, but it was warmer than the air outside, and it washed over her. It felt good against her cold, pale skin as she stepped inside.

It was quiet after the door closed. The noise of the wind and the early morning traffic on the distant highway faded. The air was thick with the chemical smell of perm solution mingled with last night's floor cleaner, filling the air of the little hair shop.

Trudy walked to the back, where the office was located. An ancient wooden coat tree sat just inside the doorway. She hung her thin navy windbreaker before hitting the bank of light switches with the flat of her hand. Rubbing her hands to chase away the cold for the umpteenth time, she wished she had the money to buy a warmer coat.

The fluorescent lights crackled as they came to life and the shop again breathed to life. The furnace was on a timer, and the fan began to purr as the furnace started to push warmer air into the six hundred and twenty-three square foot space. Rubbing her pudgy fingers together, she tried to increase her own internal temperature.

Glancing in the mirror over her station, she caught a glimpse of the middle-aged woman with brown curls falling down the sides of her full face and the rosy cheeks of her delicately applied blush. After counting her brushes and combs and checking to make sure her two electric clippers were plugged in, one for the longer cuts, the other for the finishing sideburn trims, she returned to the tiny office at the back of the shop.

Sharon had left fresh coffee in the coffeemaker's basket, just as she did every night. Trudy smiled to herself. Good girl—no, good woman, she corrected herself.

Filling the urn with water, she poured it into the coffee machine. She flipped the switch on the side of the white plastic potholder to the on position. The glow of the red light meant it was on and working. There would be fresh coffee in ten minutes. Good thing. She really needed a cup today.

She and Rocky were scheduled to meet with Mr. Simmons at the bank today. They had to renegotiate their loan repayment schedule. The hair shop had consumed most of their resources. If only Rocky would come out of his winter slumber and get a job. Once he got a job, it would really help to ease her worries about money.

Her husband complained constantly about the attitude of the townspeople toward newcomers. "They won't hire outsiders," Rocky explained.

At least for now, they had some cash flow from the shop.

This allowed them time to work out a plan with the bank before they sank below the red line into bankruptcy. Trudy sighed.

The bell over the front door tinkled. It had to be Sharon.

Exiting the office, Trudy found Sharon standing over her workstation, playing with a new brush, a replacement for the one she'd brought with her from Newport. Sharon claimed someone had stolen it off her station, but Trudy sensed Sharon had broken it or lost it somehow.

"Mornin'," said Trudy in her light, musical voice.

"Uh... hi," Sharon said, her blue-green eyes focused on the combs and brushes laid out in a neat row on the surface of her mauve-colored station. The drawer was open, which she slapped shut as soon as Trudy appeared. Her shoulder-length blonde hair, usually perfectly coiffed and combed into place, was ruffled and had a windswept look.

Sharon glanced up, and the dark circles under the woman's eyes made Trudy cringe.

"I'd like the day off. I'm not feeling well."

Trudy wondered why she hadn't just called in if she needed a day off. "Of course. Do you want me to call your appointments for today?"

"Yeah."

"Are you okay?"

Sharon shook her head. Something was obviously wrong, but if Sharon wouldn't share, there was little she could do about it.

Turning away, Sharon hurried out the front door and disappeared into the bustling mob of tourists starting their early morning shopping. Trudy watched Sharon. Her eyes were focused on the ground, causing her to almost knock over an old lady with a cane who shouted at her as she passed.

Sharon didn't meet anyone's gaze.

Walking again to the back, her rubber-soled Nike's squeaked across the tiled floor. She entered the small, whitewashed office and sat in the worn secretarial chair. Reaching out, she pulled her thin, black, nylon smock from the coat tree next to the desk.

The coffeemaker was almost finished. The hot, black liquid would feel good going down. At least their financial situation might finally begin to turn the corner.

Walking into the shop, she stopped to study Sharon's station. She considered opening the drawer, then decided not to. She made a point of not invading her employee's privacy. Trust is earned, not given, her father used to tell her when she was a girl. The new brush looked familiar, though.

Picking it up, she studied the logo. A very expensive brand, one that Sharon could never afford. Her eyes narrowed when she realized where she'd seen this before.

Rocky had bought one just like it on their last visit to the wholesale beauty supply store. She shook her head. Couldn't be. Not with all the complaining she did about her drunk of a husband. If he and Sharon—

The bell on the front door tingled brightly, breaking her train of thought. Mrs. Evanston walked through the door, grasping her heavy aluminum walker in her gnarled hands. Covering her gray hair was a thin, pale blue scarf to hold her wispy hair in place, just as she wore it every week.

Trudy glanced at her watch. 9:05. Right on the nose, as usual.

"Hello, Mrs. Evanston." Trudy forced a wide smile to her lips, though she didn't feel particularly happy at the moment.

"Hello, yourself."

Mrs. Evanston had been Trudy's first customer shortly after she'd opened for business and had been a regular ever since. She was a wily old lady of at least eighty, who only came in on seniors' discount day: Tuesday.

Mrs. Irma Evanston had married a wealthy eastern industrialist and that he died shortly after he retired and moved to Fairview.

Even if it weren't true, Mrs. Evanston was a very unpleasant and difficult person to deal with. And the cheapest woman Trudy had ever met.

"Where's Sharon?" Mrs. Evanston asked, stopping by the coat tree near the front desk long enough to remove her long, green, floor-length overcoat. Shaking the excess moisture from the coat, she pulled off a steel hanger, then used it to hang the wet coat on the rack. It would be dry before she left. Mrs. Evanston always booked an hour and a half for her roller set.

"On a day off, Trudy said, without elaborating.

Trudy glanced at the appointment book on the front desk as she passed it while helping Mrs. Evanston to the sinks where she would shampoo her hair. They would move back to Trudy's station for her to set the curlers, then Mrs. Evaston would move to one of the dryer chairs.

Odd. There were no appointments booked for Sharon today. It was the first day in the past few weeks she didn't have a least one perm and several haircuts on the schedule. It was almost as if Sharon had planned for a day off.

Trudy made a mental note to speak to Sharon about it tomorrow.

***

The day ended with Trudy doing five roller sets and five haircuts, mostly walk-ins, none by appointment. People needing haircuts, passing through tourist towns, weren't big tippers, and certainly didn't tip well enough to keep the doors open.

At five o'clock, after locking the front door as she turned to leave the store, she was nearly knocked over by a wall of man muscle.

The man, well over six feet tall, blocked her way. He smelled of motor oil, and she stared at a wide chest covered by a black tee shirt and a leather vest. Lifting her gaze, she looked up into oil-black eyes and a toothpaste smile framed by a short, scraggly beard. A thick mustache covered his upper lip and his long black hair, draped over his massive shoulders, gleamed in the fading daylight.

The evening breeze must have sprung up because Trudy shivered as the cool air washed over her.

"Uh, sorry," said Trudy.

"Are you Trudy Wilson?" asked the man mountain. His deep, resonant voice vibrated off the walls of the covered walkway.

His voice matched his size.

"Yeah." She nodded, certain she looked like a deer in the headlights of an eighteen-wheeler.

"I'm Bruce. Bruce Carstairs."

Trudy's eyes went wide. "Oh. Carstairs. You know, Sharon?"

"Yeah, she's my sister. I'm lookin' for her."

Trudy took a step back so she could see his dark eyes better. The easy smile and his thick thumbs hanging off the pockets of his faded blue jeans made him appear relaxed.

"She left early. Sick," said Trudy.

"Do you know where she lives?"

Trudy had to think about that one. Was this guy really her brother? And if he was, why didn't he know where she lived?

20

"Uh…"

He interrupted her before she could reply. "I know what you must be thinkin', who is this guy really?" Unhooking his right thumb off his front jeans pocket, he reached into his back pocket. A wallet with a stainless steel chain attached appeared in his hand. Flipping it open, he pulled out a Washington State driver's license, which he handed to her.

Studying it, she saw sure enough the license photo was his picture and the name was the one he'd given her. Handing the license back to him, she watched as he expertly slipped it inside the billfold, then stuffed the wallet back in the rear pocket of his jeans. Crossing his arms, he gave her an earnest expression.

"I can take you there if you like," she offered. At first she wondered if she should, but he seemed nice and he seemed okay.

"Okay." He nodded, his face splitting into a warm smile.

If this was what bikers were really like, then all those lurid stories on the TV were dead wrong. Swallowing, she realized her mouth was dry. *Dead wrong?*

Two

TRUDY FOLLOWED THE SWAGGERING BRUCE CARSTAIRS across the parking lot. She watched his wide butt gyrate as he walked. Stealing a glance over her shoulder behind them, she saw there were people on the covered sidewalks staring them. A guy Bruce's size clearly attracted attention.

His humming and his relaxed, causal gait said he didn't give a shit what they thought of him. He must be used to the attention.

Finally, a low-slung motorcycle came into view, parked behind a red Chevy pickup. The motorcycle had shiny chrome pipes running down the side, a large black seat, and the gas tank, which sat in front of the leather seat, was painted a royal purple. Painted on the tank was the image of a buxom, well-toned blonde in a red, barely-there bikini. The painted woman had a smile forever fixed to her face, and a twinkle fixed in the corner of both cobalt-blue eyes. Under the image, in heavily stylized yellow script, were the words "Bruce's Gal."

Bruce stopped next to the motorcycle and turned to Trudy.

"What do you think?" There was pride in his voice. She'd heard that bikers sometimes loved their bikes more than their women.

"It's very nice." Her voice sounded meek in her ears.

"Yup, she's a beaut. The other guys think she's shit, but I love my Honda."

"Why would anyone say that?"

Bruce shook his head and the smile vanished from his face. "The guys don't like rice burners, but I've had this baby since I was a kid, and I love it." Seeing trudy's puzzled expression Bruce explain rice burners were mortocycles maunfacturer in Japan. The real motorcycle men rode Harley Davidson's.

"Guys?" Trudy could imagine whom he was talking about, but she didn't have the nerve to ask. This guy was big and scary. Still, he seemed kind of friendly, like a big teddy bear.

"You wanna a ride?" Bruce asked, ignoring her question.

"No. I have my car over there." Trudy pointed toward her old, rusted-out red two-door Chevette. The irony of the color of original paint had never been lost on her, since rust was the only thing holding the car together these days. But at least it's paid for, she thought. "Follow me. It's easy to get lost on the back roads around here," she said, offering him a thin-lipped smile.

"Yeah, okay. You know, you're all right." He grinned.

Stepping up next to his bike, he grabbed the helmet hanging off the passenger bar at the back of the seat. Slipping it over his head with the strap under his chin, he adjusted the helmet over his long, jet-black hair, which ran poker straight down his bull neck, then down his back. The trails of hair stuck from beneath the helmet's brim like a river. She had never seen a man's hair that long before. It was almost a work of art.

Trudy went to her car. Reaching into her purse, she grabbed the key with the GM logo. It slid easily into the lock and there was an audible click as she turned it.

She tugged, and the door flew open, the hinges protesting loudly with an ear-splitting crunch of rusted metal. As she climbed in, she heard the roar of a motorcycle engine come to life and the deep throbbing rumble as it began to move. Looking down, she slipped the key into the ignition and turned it. The engine coughed and sputtered once, then began to run in its usual jumpy, misfiring way.

She called the car her red, rusted, piece of shit, or POS for short. But then, it did get her around town, if not in the style she would have preferred.

The rumble of the motorcycle engine increased until Bruce, sitting astride the powerful purple monster, rolled up beside her. Grinning, he signaled with a thumbs-up for her to lead the way.

Glancing in the rearview mirror, she backed up, turned, and headed for the street behind the mall. Darkness had crept across the sky, leaving a dusting of stars, so she switched on the headlights. The twin beams cut through the gloom.

At the green light where the side street met Highway 101, she turned left and headed south. One quick glance back told her that Bruce was right behind her—at a safe distance, of course.

They passed the real estate office, the town's small library, and Bill's Independent Grocers as they drove along the two-lane highway.

Soon they arrived at Bard Street, where she made a right turn. Bruce stayed with her. They rounded the curve in the road and the ocean came into view. She could see that the white-capped waves were about six feet high today. Foam-topped walls of green water were rushing toward the pure, finely pounded sand of the long beach. The ocean would be very cold. No swimming.

They drove to the bottom of the hill until they came to the sign for Spirit Road.

Sharon shared a rented house with a couple of other girls. Trudy had only been down here a couple of times, so it took her a few moments to find the correct house.

It was a three-bedroom beach house. Probably someone's old summer place, back in the sixties, now a rental. Trudy and Rocky had stayed in a house like this when they first moved to town, until they found more permanent accommodation. The house they ended up buying was pretty much a fixer-upper, which Rocky had promised he would fix up before he snagged a full time job. That had been six months ago, and the house still remained more of a fixer than an upper. He'd been too busy he said to find work. Yeah right, drinking and oogling the female barflys was all he did.

The brakes squeaked when she stopped the car in front of the little gray house with the blue wooden weather shutters with little hearts carved in them. In front was a flower garden with a ceramic gnome wearing a green hat, red curl-toed shoes, a white open-necked shirt, and a green vest and cherry red pants. The flowers were mostly dead sticks. Trudy guessed the girls who lived here weren't the gardening type.

Bruce pulled in behind her. She turned off the engine, and his motorcycle engine went silent immediately. Flipping the stand down with one booted foot, he eased the bike's weight onto the kickstand.

After dismounting, he stood beside the bike. Slipping the helmet off his head, he flipped his hair over his shoulder as he strode to the driver's side window of her car. The window squealed as she rolled it down.

"This it?" he asked.

"Yeah. She shares it."

Bruce nodded, and with the helmet swinging from two thick, meaty fingers, started toward the pale peach front door.

Starting the car's little engine again, Trudy looked behind her and backed up, when she suddenly stood on the brake pedal after spotting a familiar vehicle out of the corner of one eye. She swiveled in her seat to stare at the navy blue pickup truck parked down the street a couple of hundred yards away. It looked familiar. There didn't appear to be anyone inside the cab, at least that she could see through the rear window. She studied the license plate. It wasn't Rocky's, but it sure looked like his truck. What the hell would he be doing here, anyway? She shrugged and rolled up the car's window.

She stepped on the gas pedal. The little car sputtered its way to the corner, where she turned and headed back up the hill.

***

After Trudy's car disappeared over the crest of the hill, a lone figure sat up from behind the steering wheel of the blue truck. A reflection of stray light revealed two eyes that had been watching the little Chevette until it disappeared. After the echo of the sputtering engine died away, the shadowy figure started the engine of the pickup. It roared to life and the truck drove slowly toward the hill, its headlights off.

***

It was nearly five thirty when Rocky Wilson pulled his blue pickup into the empty parking stall in front of the Whaler Bar and Grill off 38th Street in Fairview next door to Rob's Books. He planned to meet Sharon here.

He shivered with sexual excitement as he thought about her soft, voluptuous young body in his arms.

They had been lovers three times in the last month, and each time seemed like the first. It was almost as if the past twenty years had disappeared. He was a stud again. A sexual dynamo. Her flowing blonde hair and moans of ecstasy rang in his ears as he remembered their last meeting.

He didn't see her car anywhere, but it was only 5:25, so she still had five minutes.

He turned off the engine and stepped out of his truck. The door squealed on its hinges in protest. Pushing it shut, he paused to look in the side view mirror at his neatly trimmed beard. After flashing his best, twisted smile, he strode toward the double oak doors leading into the smoke-filled bar. His brown leather ankle boots were polished to a high shine, the first time he'd bothered to make the effort in years.

His checkered sport coat hung open over his neatly pressed blue jeans, held up by a black belt, which strained to hold his pants up as his potbelly spilled over the waistband.

At the doors to the bar, he gripped the large, ornately carved brass handle of the right door, swung it open, then entered.

His vision quickly adjusted to the dim interior as he strode toward the bar. The low-slung, black metal lampshades cast spotlights over the booths along the outer edge, and the solid, dark wood tables, each with four matching captain's chairs, sat in the center of the room. On each table was a lit candle inside a pale orange glass vase. The tables were covered with sheets of glass to make cleaning spills easier.

Against the wall farthest from the doors was the thirty-foot-long teak bar. It was polished to a high shine, reflecting the light from the low-wattage bulbs in the metal lamps over the tables.

Kelly, the red-haired New York escapee bartender, stood behind the bar in his white, open-necked shirt, his navy vest unbuttoned as usual. He was having an animated conversation with Harold Schultz, one of the many regular barflys that frequented the place.

Rocky walked straight to the bar. Kelly's freckled face broke into a wide grin when he noticed him.

"Rock, how you doin'?" Marks had dropped into silence when Rocky appeared, but didn't look at him, preferring to stare into his glass of whiskey as if studying its smoky aroma.

"Good. Thanks, Kelly. You seen Sharon?"

"Nope. She meetin' you here again?" Kelly winked at him.

"Uh... yeah." Rocky's eyes shifted to the bar top as he reached into his back pocket for his wallet. Pulling out a single, he slapped it on the bar. "You got change for a one? I gotta make a call."

"Sure," said Kelly. Picking up the one-dollar bill, he turned to the register underneath the large mirror that reflected the row of liquor bottles on shelves in front of the mirror. The register bell chimed brightly as the cash drawer opened.

Kelly flipped up the bill holder; after placing the single in the slot, he extracted four quarters, then pushed the drawer closed with his right hip in an oft-practiced move.

He placed the four twenty-five cent pieces on the bar. "There you go," he said, a knowing smile on his face.

Picking up the quarters, Rocky nodded at Kelly, then headed for the front doors. He could have used one of the pay phones in the corridor leading to the washrooms, but he decided to go outside to use the phone booth at the corner store next door for maximum privacy. He wanted to use his cell phone, but Trudy might see the bill and the numbers he called.

I may be a drunk, but I'm not stupid.

28

***

After the door closed behind Rocky, Marks shared his opinion about what they'd just seen. "That stupid son of a bitch is really gonna git himself in deep shit one of these days. The way I hear it, that little whore eats guys like him for breakfast."

Kelly nodded grimly, then the two men continued with their earlier conversation. The pending baseball trades were a far more interesting topic than Rocky Wilson's love life.

Three

BRUCE KNOCKED ON THE FRONT DOOR of his sister's house until finally a long-legged brunette answered. She wore tight-fitting black jeans, which accented her tight butt and shapely hips. Her long, flowing dark hair rested on her bare shoulders. The tight red tube top she wore barely contained her firm, nicely rounded breasts. In her scarlet-fingernailed right hand, she carried a lit cigarette that emitted a trail of thin, gray smoke. The smoke followed her as she moved.

Her dark eyes sparkled when she saw Bruce standing on the doorstep.

"Why hello, handsome. What can I do for you?"

"Hi. I'm Bruce Carstairs. Sharon's brother. Is she here?"

"Nope. She's out at the store. Wanna come in and wait?"

"Sure," Bruce said, nodding.

Stepping aside to let him pass, she took a hit from her cigarette. After exhaling, she said, "My name's Emily, but everyone one calls me Sparkle because I'm the life of the party. You wanna party?" Lowering her head, she looked up at him through the veil of her flowing hair; her eyes giving him that bedroom look he'd seen many times before.

Bruce smiled at her, then walked into the living room. A large, gray, overstuffed couch sat against one wall, facing a large picture window that offered a view of the bay beyond the trees across the street. On the opposite wall sat a matching chair. Through the window, he could see the spectacular boiling water pounding into the beige-colored sand. The sound of the pounding, crashing surf could be heard through the glass.

The scarred hardwood floor creaked underfoot as he crossed the room. Several pictures interrupted the bare white walls while along one wall was a bookcase that held no books, but did have a collection of seashells in various shapes and colors.

"Naw. Maybe later," he said.

She looked momentarily disappointed, then followed him inside. "Have a seat," she said, waving one slender, tanned arm toward the couch. She stubbed her cigarette out in the glass ashtray on the coffee table.

As he sat down on the couch, his bulk sank into the soft cushions. He wasn't sure if he would be able to get out again without help. He studied the room. There wasn't much in it. In one corner was a small television with a set of old-fashioned bunny ears resting on top. No cable. He supposed these girls weren't big TV watchers.

She padded across the room, her knitted slippers cushioning the sound of her footsteps. Sliding the final distance, she landed in the chair on her butt and threw her long legs over the chair arm. One arm rested in her lap, while the other rested on the side of her head. Her dark eyes were fixed on his.

Resting his palms flat on his thighs, he said, "So. You share this place with my sister?"

"Yup, me and another girl. Alice. She's at work. Won't be home until after eleven."

Emily licked her lips as if they were dry, causing an involuntary stirring in his groin. She was a sexy girl and knew how to use all the weapons in her arsenal. Her gentle perfume enveloped him like a cloud of heavenly fragrance, as if the jasmine were trying to carry him away. He cleared his mind. He wasn't here to fuck; he was here to see Sharon. Maybe later he'd take Sparkle up on her offer, but not now.

The sound of squealing brakes being applied, hard, on the street outside interrupted his thoughts. He heard a car engine being turned off, followed by a heavy metal door being slammed.

The front door burst open and Sharon appeared, running through the door, causing it to bang violently against the wall. She ran straight for Bruce.

She greeted him by leaping into his arms with tears streaming down her face, her makeup running down her cheeks. He hugged her to him tightly. Her body was trembling.

"Bruce... oh Bruce..." was all she managed to say as she sobbed uncontrollably.

Wrapping his arms around her, he cooed her name, rocking her like a baby even though he was the younger of the two. "There, there…"

He unwound one hand from around her to hold her head against his shoulder; he felt her hot tears begin to seep through the fabric of his tee shirt.

"Tell me what's wrong," he said, his voice gentle.

Emily had left the room. He heard the sound of a tap being turned on, accompanied by the echo of running water from the kitchen, visible just off the living room. He guessed Emily was making tea. Good call. He liked tea.

The bikers he worked for would have laughed at him, but his late maternal grandmother had served an excellent brew. He'd enjoyed tea ever since.

With Emily in the other room, it would give him alone time with Sis to see what the hell she'd been up to. And what sort of trouble she was in this time.

Sharon's pleading azure pools stared back at him when she lifted her head from his shoulder to gaze into his eyes. Her eyes were red, no doubt from crying for a long time.

"I need to sleep," she said, then buried her head again in his shoulder and whimpered like she had when she was little. Holding her close, he gently rocked her.

Within seconds, her breathing slowed and he felt the rise and fall of her body as her breathing became even. Her eyes were closed. She was about to drift off.

Emily reappeared from the kitchen with a steaming coffee cup in her right hand. Seeing Sharon drifting off, Emily nodded toward the hallway leading off the front room to indicate where the bedrooms were.

Bruce shuffled forward on the couch cushion, lifting Sharon's limp body in his arms. Raising himself to his feet, he cradled his sister's weight his arms and carried her toward the hallway and the bedrooms.

Emily mouthed, "The second one on the left is Sharon's."

Once there, he used the toe of his right boot to ease the door open. The room smelled of rose water and jasmine and was very dark. There was a bed pushed against the wall.

The bed was covered with a white, knitted-shawl bedspread, and two large, fluffy pillows crushed against the brass headboard.

There were two brown teddy bears sitting atop the pillows, their black eyes staring back at him. They were like sentinels, guarding her sanctuary.

Bruce laid Sharon's now sleeping form on the bed as if she were a small child. Immediately she turned her back to him and curled into a fetal position.

Edging toward the door, he gently closed it after him and returned to the living room.

Emily, aka Sparkle, was waiting for him, sitting with one leg folded under the other on the couch, sipping from the coffee cup. The string from a tea bag hung over the side of the cup.

"Problems?" she asked, with an innocent expression on her face.

Bruce nodded and sighed heavily. "Probably guy trouble, as usual." He sat in the chair across from the comely brunette. "I guess I'll have to bail her out again."

"You killed a guy for her once, didn't you?" asked Sparkle.

He swore her eyes smoked with excitement and passion. She must be the type who loves the bad boys.

Bruce chuckled grimly. "There's a lot more to that story. Sharon has a way of blowing this shit up to be more than it is."

Sparkle looked momentarily disappointed, then her face brightened to a smile. "Why don't we fuck while we wait?"

The direct approach—he liked that. Where did Sharon find babes like this as roommates? "Okay," he said with a shrug, "why not."

Giggling, she placed her cup on the glass end table, then leapt to her feet, rushed over to him, grabbed his hand, and pulled him up. Brought to his feet again, she led him down the hall toward her bedroom.

Four

TRUDY PARKED HER CHEVETTE ON THE DRIVEWAY in front of her house. She and Rocky had bought it as a fixer-upper, but she loved it. The old, single pane windows rattled something fierce when the wind blew, particularly during the winter storms, but that added to the house's charm.

Rocky should have had most of the remodeling done by now, but his love of beer had grown since they moved to Fairview. He'd always been a drinker, but he had never drunk as much as he did now. He practically lived at the Whaler Bar and Grill these days.

Stepping out of the car, she realized her knees had begun to ache. Similarly, her back felt like she'd been lifting bags of bricks all day long, not standing cutting hair for eight hours. She hoped her body would hold out longer than their money.

When Rocky sold his auto parts supply business to move here and set her up in the shop, they had thought they had all the money they would ever need. At the time, two hundred and fifty thousand dollars seemed more than enough.

Doris Moscow sold her the shop for eighty thousand, but the real value was her client list—at least, that's what Trudy had been told.

Doris had moved to Chicago to live with her sister and be nearer her grandchildren.

Her local clients certainly weren't going to follow her there. Unfortunately, most locals weren't about to place their faith in a newcomer, so Trudy's business had a slow start and their cash reserves were quickly dwindling.

Sharon Carstairs had seemed to be a godsend when she arrived at the shop and immedaitley attracted a good sized client lsit ina very short time. The word of mouth network on the coast was amazing when you saw it in action. Today's small take proved just how much Sharon meant to the continued success of the shop. Trudy only brought in one hundred dollars today. A string of one-hundred-dollar days like this one would soon mean the end of the business.

Trudy thought she better call Sharon to see if she was okay.

After unlocking the front door of the house, she stepped inside, closing the door after her. The odor of the fresh salmon she had cooked yesterday greeted her. Slipping off her low-rise shoes, she wiggled her toes in the old, long, green shag carpet. She sighed. Surprising how good taking off her shoes felt.

It was wonderful to be home. She flicked one of the three white switches beside the front door and a light came on, illuminating the cramped entry way.

She opened one of the sliding wooden closet doors to her right, where she kept the coats and shoes. Their heavy winter coats hung neatly, and a row of men and women's shoes of various styles were lined up, like soldiers standing in review formation. She slipped her windbreaker off, hung it up, and closed the door.

Moving to the three switches, she flicked the middle one and the light above the stairs leading to the upper floor of the split-level house lit up the carpeted stairs.

She picked up the mail lying on the tiled floor before heading up the stairs. There were three envelopes today. Scanning the envelopes, she walked up the five stairs to the living room.

At the top, she stopped. One envelope was from a bank, wanting them to apply for a credit card; another was the power company bill; but the third had their address handwritten in blue ink on a white, letter-sized envelope. There was no return address. The postmark was from the post office in Newport.

She flicked the switch on the wall and the chandelier in the living room came on. There was a wood-framed couch with green cushions in front of the windows overlooking the street. There were only five other houses on this road.

The quiet of the neighborhood had been a deciding factor for Trudy when they purchased the house.

The well-used floor-to-ceiling stone fireplace stood against one wall; it would get a workout tonight. She planned to curl up in the gray leather recliner. Beside it stood the brown metal reading lamp, stiffly hovering over the recliner. It was a good place to curl up to read the latest spy thriller or steamy romance novel she enjoyed.

When Rocky came home, he disappeared into the room they'd set aside with the guys' toys with all the buttons. He sat in there for hours, drinking beer, watching TV, or playing his music on the expensive stereo he'd insisted on buying before they moved here. He hadn't been home much lately, at least until very late most nights, so her suggestion that the thing was a waste of money seemed to be proving itself correct. Not that he'd give a shit what she thought.

Throwing the mail on the brown-stained pine coffee table, she walked into the adjoining kitchen. The room had few modern conveniences: a simple electric stove and twenty-year-old refrigerator, in different colors.

At least the long, cove-top faux wood counters gave her plenty of room for food preparation, not that she did much of that these days. No one visited them.

The white-flecked tile on the floor gleamed from the last mop and wax she had given them. Padding on bare feet to the fridge, she swung the dark brown door open. The appliances were old but they kept on chugging. The bare light bulb inside revealed a few cans of beer on the top shelf next to the half pint of creamer. On one of the mostly empty three shelves was a plastic bag containing two lemons, the plastic container with the remaining fish that would be her dinner tonight, and a bag of pre-made salad.

She pulled out the fish container, the bag of mixed salad, and the bottle of Italian dressing.

After placing the cold fish on a white Pyrex plate from the cupboard over the counter next to the fridge, she opened the salad bag along the zipper lock. She piled a stack of salad and drizzled some dressing over it. Opening a drawer, she got herself a dinner fork.

Picking up the plate, she moved to one of the matching pine chairs around the kitchen table and sat down. She ate her meal as she scanned the envelopes.

She tossed the credit card pitch aside without opening it. With the fingers of her left hand, she tore off one end of the envelope of the power bill, extracted the contents, then flipped the folded bill flat on the table. After scanning the charges, she relaxed. She could pay this month. That would be nice.

Lastly, she studied the handwriting on the plain white envelope. The address was scrawled as if it had been written in haste. Her name and the address were clear enough, but the zip code was jumbled and almost unreadable.

After putting down her fork, she chewed the salmon slowly and used both hands to open the envelope. Inside was a folded, single sheet of plain white paper.

She unfolded the paper and saw the same style of writing as on the envelope. As she read, she stopped chewing.

The room began to spin and she nearly lost the food in her mouth as her stomach heaved. Her eyes widened and her heart beat hard and rapidly in her chest.

That son of a bitch was having an affair. She'd had no idea that he was doing this before now, before today.

The note said simply, Rocky and Sharon are sleeping together. There was no signature.

Pushing her plate away, dark thoughts crept across her mind. What would she do? Was it true? Could it be? Confront Rocky? Or Sharon? Or both of them? What about her business? Would she lose everything?

She owed Sharon. Damn the slut—she owed her. *What a fucking mess.*

Five

ROCKY PICKED UP THE TELEPHONE RECEIVER, then slipped a quarter into the slot of the pay phone. Headlights from passing cars illuminated the glass of the phone booth. The accordion door of the booth muffled the street noise. The air felt heavy and smelled of rain.

The phone jangled as the coin disappeared. He dialed Sharon's number and waited, as there was a series of clicks until the phone at the other end began to ring. After two rings, a feminine voice answered.

"Hello?" The voice wasn't Sharon's.

"Hi, it's Rocky. Is Sharon there?"

"Nope. She went to the grocery store."

Rocky felt a twinge of impatience rising inside him. Sharon always seemed to be out whenever he called, and her roommates never offered to take a message. Getting information out of either of them was always a lot of work, and he was tired of trying. Bitches.

"Let her know I called, will you?"

"Yeah." The line went dead.

He paused before hanging up. Why would she be at the store if she were supposed to be here with him? *Another man*?

A flash of anger crossed his mind. She's a slut plain and simple. What the hell did he expect?

Slamming the receiver into the holder, he pushed the accordion door aside in order to exit the phone booth. A cold rain had begun to fall, small drops at first, about to become heavier in the next few minutes. It rained so much on the coast he thought sometimes it was a wonder he hadn't grown webs between his toes.

He headed back for the entrance to the Whaler. Might as well have a few drinks to drown his misery. Trudy would be home by now, but so what?

***

Bruce heard Sparkle's breathing become regular and soft. Good, she was asleep. He would head back to the Overlook Motel, where he'd left his stuff. Sparkle said he could stay with them while he was in town. Seeing as she was kinda fun, he thought it would be a good idea to take her up on her offer.

Moving cat-like, he made his way to the bedroom door, then slipped into the hall. He'd carried his Daytons out of Sparkle's room so his boots wouldn't make their usual clunky sounds. He didn't want to wake anyone up.

Moving along to Sharon's bedroom door, he froze when an ear-splitting scream startled him. This was followed by something striking him on back of the head.

"Owwww!" Dropping to his knees, he covered his head with his arms as blows continued to rain down on him. "Hey! What the fuck?" he protested.

"Take that you...." It was a woman's voice. One he didn't recognize. He hoped it was the other roommate, Alice.

41

If she wasn't Alice, then he was in real trouble.

"Alice, stop, please! I'm Sharon's brother," he said.

The sound of his sister's name had the desired effect and the blows stopped. Suddenly a bright light came on, illuminating the hallway and momentarily blinding him.

"Really?" the voice said.

His vision cleared enough so he could make out a tall, lithe blonde, wearing a floor-length flannel nightgown and holding a teddy bear the size of a small dog over her head, ready to strike another blow. Her hair was braided into pigtails that fell down the sides of her head, and her gray-green eyes were wide.

"Yeah. Really." He stood on shaky legs.

"Sorry. I didn't know. Sparkle and Sharon don't let guys sleep over—usually."

"Yeah, well, Sparkle asked me to stay here while I'm in town. You okay with that, Alice?"

She nodded, then lowered the brown teddy bear to her side, where it hung by one arm. The stuffed bear had black eyes and had a cherry-red ribbon around its neck.

"I'll just check on Sharon and then go get my stuff," said Bruce.

Her eyes were focused on the floor. "Okay. I guess I'll go back to bed." Turning, she walked to the door at the end of the hallway. The hall light remained on. Glancing back at him over her shoulder, she offered him a tight smile before she closed her bedroom door.

Bruce shook his head. Gingerly he used his fingers to find the spot on his head where she had been hitting him. He winced when he located a small, painful bump where one of the hard button eyes had struck. *Bitch doesn't know her own strength.*

Easing Sharon's bedroom door open, he slipped inside and closed the door as soundlessly as possible behind him.

The only light came from the streetlamp outside her window. There weren't the usual sleeping sounds, so he moved to the bed. He made out rumpled bedsheets but no sign of Sharon. Even the telltale smell of her perfume was missing.

He paused to think. He didn't recall hearing her door closing from inside Emily's room, but then he'd been a little busy to hear much of anything over the girl's moans. Smiling, he recalled how passionate she had been. The girl was a real wildcat.

But where could Sharon be? He pressed the button on his digital watch and the watch face lit up. It was after one in the morning.

Slipping quietly out of her room, he went to the living room. Her coat and shoes were gone from the shoe rack in the entryway. Pulling the plastic blinds on the front window aside with one hand, he saw her car was gone, too. His bike stood there, untouched, right where he'd left it.

Reaching into his vest pocket, he found his keys. The skull-shaped knob on the key ring grinned at him. Just when he'd found his sister, he'd lost her again; he'd been too busy, too absorbed in his own pleasure.

Son of a bitch, he cursed himself.

After slipping on his boots, he unlocked the dead bolt on the front door, went outside, and soon straddled his motorcycle. A strong wind blew sea air into his lungs and was accompanied by the sound of the surf attacking the sandy shore in the darkness. Flipping up the steel stand with his right foot, he slipped the key into the ignition and turned it. He pressed the electric starter button on the right handle bar and the powerful motorcycle engine sprang to life, drowning out the crash of the coastal waves. Revving the engine twice, he released the clutch and the bike leapt forward like it was a lion unleashed upon its prey.

The engine roared and soon he steered the motorcycle onto the street, gunned the engine, and started up the hill. He had to find his sister. Instinctively, he knew her disappearing in the middle of the night was a bad thing. And he knew just where to start looking for her.

***

Trudy sat alone at the slate gray arborite-covered kitchen table, staring at the glass of white Chardonnay. The stem rested on a green knit place mat like three others, sitting in front of the other chairs around the table. She smiled at the thought of how she always sat alone in the evenings. No one, not even her husband of fifteen years, would sit with her.

A single tear escaped her right eye to run down her cheek. It fell from her cheek to land on her heavy purple flannel nightgown, where it disappeared into the fabric. Both eyes welled with tears.

Where had she gone wrong? Why had Rocky strayed? Wasn't she attractive enough or exciting enough for him anymore? She remembered their early years together and how they had made love at the drop of a hat.

That had all changed when she'd had the two miscarriages and the hysterectomy. He'd become distant, but continued to say he loved her and always would. He'd lied. She patted her little potbelly. Maybe I'm fat?

The doorbell rang, interrupting her thoughts.

Sliding back the chair, she giggled. She realized she was getting a little tipsy.

Swallowing her giggles, she managed to weave her way down the stairs to the front door.

Squinting through the peephole, she saw a black shirt standing on her front step. She opened the door a crack without disengaging the security chain.

"Who is it?"

"Bruce Carstairs. We met earlier today?"

Momentarily, she wondered why he was here, and how he had found her. He was her brother. Anger flared from deep inside her.

"I don't know where she is. Now leave me alone." Her voice betrayed the bitterness she felt.

"Is something wrong?" he asked.

She slammed the door shut with enough force to make the metallic gold doorknocker slap once against the wood with a dull thud and slapped the switch with the palm of her hand, turning off the porch light. She wanted no part of Sharon or her brother.

***

Bruce shook his head, then retreated to the driveway. The light in the stairwell of the two story split-level house went dark as well. The light from behind the closed living room curtains stayed on.

Bruce considered his options, shrugged, then straddled his bike again. He started the motor, kicked the stand into place, and then pushed the bike backward with his feet until he was on the gravel road. The collection of smooth stones crunched like dry breakfast cereal underneath the tires of the motorcycle. He flicked the clutch lever and gave the motor gas. He sped away, leaving a trail of smoky dust in his wake until he and his motorized steed were swallowed by the night.

Six

I~N~ H~IS~ D~RUNKEN~ S~TUPOR~, Rocky wobbled in the phone booth outside the Whaler. He'd closed one eye and managed to slip a quarter into the coin slot. A sense of pride filled him when he managed to dial her number. I not only drive better drunk, I dial better, too. He snorted at his joke.

After a click and a short pause, the phone on the other end of the line rang loudly in his ear. Rocky's mouth was dry. He ran his tongue around his lips. The taste of stale beer and cigarettes was all that remained of the evening. Through the fog in his mind, he wondered what he would say to the bitch. She had stood him up too often. She had to pay for what she'd done with his heart. He decided to dump her, yeah, that's what he'd do.

Lifting the receiver from the cradle, it seemed heavier than before. He managed to keep himself upright by leaning against the glass-and-aluminum wall of the phone booth.

On the third ring, a woman's voice answered.

"Yeah?"

"Hi, iss Rocky." He struggled to keep the slur from his speech. He sounded pretty good to his own ears.

"Hi, Rocky. This is Sparkle."

Rocky recalled the little brunette with the mean ass and smiled. Maybe he'd bed her next. Sharon said he was a great lover.

"Hi, Sparkle. Is Sharon d'ere?" He put a hand over his mouth to suppress a burp.

"Actually, no, she's at the store." Her voice sounded musical and he thought the little bitch might be laughing at him. Cradling the receiver under his chin, he raised his right hand to look at his watch. The numbers weren't entirely clear, but they looked like they might be telling him it was after midnight. What store was open in this town after midnight? None that he knew of, that much was certain. He decided to sound like he couldn't care less where Sharon had gone.

"Okay… tell her I called… tell her I'll call… later."

"Okay." The line went dead.

Rocky placed the receiver back in its cradle and reached for the handle for the folding door of the booth. Trying to move it, he failed until he used both hands to push it back. He stumbled out, nearly falling on his face before he managed to catch himself. The world is uneven, he decided.

Reaching into the right pocket of his checkered sport coat, he found his keys and looked around the parking lot for his truck. There were two vehicles remaining in the lot in front of the Whaler. By its shape, one had to be his truck. The other had to be a taxi because it had a light box on the roof.

Stumbling toward what he thought was his truck, he willed his wobbley legs to keep moving. Come on baby, we can make it.

When he got beside the driver's door, he closed one bloodshot eye and aimed the key carefully into the lock.

As he turned the lock, the lights on the car beside him began to flash red, blue, and white, forcing him to shield his eyes. He realized the car wasn't a taxi.

Cops. Fuckin' cops.

***

Bruce stopped his bike on the concrete driveway of Sharon's house. His dufflebag hung off the chrome roll bar on the seat behind him. He'd brought two changes of underwear and a second black tee shirt. He hadn't expected to stay more than the weekend before he returned home to Federal Way and his job in Seattle at Bikers Ride Forever. He'd have to call Charlie in the morning to let him know he'd be gone a little longer than he'd originally planned.

Charlie would blow a gasket—literally. Month-end was coming and he needed Bruce to ensure the books were in order for the accountant. He sighed. It couldn't be helped.

With the kickstand in place, he left the bike in the rain and started for the front door. Once he got a raincoat, he'd find something to cover the bike with. Cold drops of rain, buoyed by a strong wind, struck him in the face. Bowing his head, he rushed to get inside. The strap of the black, waterproof bag with the Harley Davidson logo on one side was slung over his right shoulder.

Climbing the two cement steps to the door, he was about to grasp the large, ornate metal doorknob and use the key Sparkle had given him, when the door suddenly flew open in front of him. He wondered who would still be up at this hour. Surprisingly, it was Sparkle, holding the door open. She waved him inside.

"Thanks," he said as he stepped through the open door. He felt as if he should shake himself like his black lab, Oscar, did when he wanted to rid himself of excess moisture. He felt a twinge as he recalled the happy, playful dog with its long tail wagging at him. He hoped Charlie was treating Oscar okay.

"Sharon's missing," said Emily, her dark eyes serious, a frown creasing her brow.

"Missing?" he asked. One thing his big sister was good at it was taking care of herself.

"Aren't you listening?" Emily crossed her arms and went into the living room. He followed behind her, a puzzled expression on his face.

"Sparkle." He hoped to calm her by using her nickname. "Sharon's out partying somewhere." That was Sharon's way of saying she was fucking some guy, but it was something he didn't like to think. But he had to admit she'd always used sex as a weapon when it came to guys and he didn't want to know the details about some of the things she'd done to get what she wanted.

"You don't understand." Emily plunked herself crossed-legged on the couch. She stuck out her bottom lip like some pouty kid.

He smiled. "If you mean you, then no, I don't. If you're talking about my sister, then I think I've known her longer than you have and she's never missing for long. What makes you think this is different?"

Emily sighed heavily and let her bare arms fall to her sides. She was wearing a red see-through teddy. She wasn't wearing a bra and Bruce could see the brown areolas on her full breasts through the sheer fabric. He could also see the outline of a pair of white panties. On her feet, she wore a pair of fuzzy bunny slippers.

With floppy ears and cheery, beady button eyes that stared back at him and made him smile slightly.

"She told me she would be back in an hour after she broke up with one of her boyfriends, only she's not back yet."

So that's where she went, thought Bruce. He moved to sit beside Sparkle on the couch, wrapped one muscular arm over her shoulders, and pulled her close. He caught the scent of her light cinnamon perfume mixed with soap.

Glancing at his watch, he said, "Listen, it's almost five in the morning now; we need some sleep. How about we get some shut-eye, then in the morning when we wake up, we see if she's back. What do you say?"

Emily lowered her head and pushed it into his shoulder to snuggle against him. Her body heat transferred to him through his cold, damp clothes.

"Hey," she started. "You're all wet and cold."

He nodded. "Yeah, it started raining." He indicated the picture window. The sky was beginning to brighten as night began its slow retreat, the eastern sky getting steadily brighter.

"Let's get you to the bedroom and get those wet things off. We can snuggle and warm you up, okay?" Her eyes turned up to gaze into his and he saw the flame of lust beginning its slow burn once more.

He shrugged. "Yeah."

They rose as one from the couch, their arms still around each other's shoulders, and began a slow walk toward her bedroom. She slid her arm down to his butt and gave him a playful squeeze as they closed the bedroom door behind them.

It would be another hour before they finally drifted off to sleep.

Seven

THE SUN ROSE, SENDING ITS RAYS THROUGH THE MORNING MIST and causing it to disperse. Little clouds of steam danced above the wet pavement outside the blue-and-gray bungalow, like ghosts rising into the crisp morning air.

The sound of a shower running, the hard spray striking naked flesh, could be heard through the thin walls of the bungalow. Bruce hummed a nonsensical tune from his childhood as he applied sweet-smelling shampoo to his long, wet hair. In the small kitchen, Emily stood over a black cast-iron frying pan, watching two pools of clear egg whites beginning to turn white around two yellow yolks.

Bruce turned off the water, wrung his hair, then stepped out onto the fine cotton towel he'd brought into the bathroom with him. He quickly dried his body with a matching towel. Next, he cupped the long, dark train of shiny hair in the fold of the towel and squeezed excess water from the strands. It would be at least three hours before it was completely dry, but he felt refreshed and even awake after a night of limited sleep.

Pulling on his blue jockeys, he applied deodorant and then tugged on his only other black tee shirt.

He tossed his damp hair over his shoulder, then pulled out a wide-toothed comb and ran it through his hair.

He stepped into his black jeans, then glanced into the fogged mirror. Running a hand over the glass to clear it, he saw he needed a shave. The stubble of dark beard was becoming prominent on his cheeks and chin.

Reaching inside the nylon pack he'd tossed into a chair, he retrieved his electric shaver. He mowed his stubble until he was satisfied with the somewhat clean face that looked back at him from the mirror. His light complexion and jet-black hair often made his skin appear dirty. Sometimes he thought he should shave twice a day, but he hated doing it even once.

He finished by brushing his teeth. The taste of the mint-flavored gel that he'd found in the mirrored cabinet over the sink wasn't his usual brand, but as often happened when he traveled, he'd forgotten some minor toiletry item.

He rinsed his mouth, cleaned the sink, then opened the bathroom door and entered the hallway.

As he passed Sharon's closed bedroom door, he paused, thinking he might knock, then shook his head. No, he decided, he better let her sleep off troubles. He hoped she'd made it home early this morning while he'd been asleep. Placing one ear on the door, he imagined he heard her snoring. He knew Sparkle was wrong about his sister. She always made it home.

Alice's door was open when he passed. He glanced inside and saw her bed neatly made, with a knitted, multi-colored afghan thrown across the bedspread. Squares of the afghan were black, fire engine red, lime green, and sky blue. Perched atop the pillows was a large, white teddy bear, its eyes smiling back at him.

Bruce smiled back. Alice didn't seem the type to be living with girls like Sparkle and Sharon. She seemed more small-town girl-next-door than a let's-party big-city girl.

Arriving in the kitchen, his senses were greeted by the smell of frying bacon and toast. Emily stood over the stove, a spatula in her hand; with her back to him, her full concentration was on the frying pan. She was wearing a sleeveless top that bared her midriff, tight blue jeans, and wooden sandals. Bruce came up behind her and wrapped his muscular arms around her slender body to cup her heavy breasts with his large hands.

"Hey, buddy, what do you think you're doin'?" Her voice teased but she didn't resist.

"Just testing to see if they're both the same size."

"Well, not right now, please, I'm busy," she said in mock protest.

Releasing her warm flesh, Bruce moved to the little kitchen table with two mismatched vinyl chairs on either side. The table had cigarette burn marks scarring the surface and looked to him like a fifties-era antique.

Sitting in one of the chairs, he set his hands flat on the tabletop.

"Where's my breakfast, woman?" he asked in a mocking tone.

Emily giggled. It was the first time she'd let her guard down around him. Even when they had been sharing spit, he'd sensed her caution. It was as if she was afraid to let her true feelings show. Now she was like a little girl. For the first time, he wondered how old she really was.

Moving to the upper cupboards beside the stove, she pulled out an ivory-white dinner plate. She slid the eggs onto the plate with three pieces of crisp bacon from another frying pan. On the counter next to the shiny, stainless steel two-slice toaster was a small, green side plate with two slices of toast on it.

Picking up the two plates, she delivered them to him at the table. After placing the food in front of him, she walked to another cupboard near the sink, where she pulled out a large ceramic coffee mug. On the side were the words "Love is Forever" in large, stylized lettering. She filled it with black coffee from the coffeemaker.

"Got any milk and sugar?" he asked, looking around the kitchen. She nodded toward the fridge; he started to rise from his chair when she smiled and waved at him to remain seated.

Her sandals echoed on the tiled floor as she walked to the fridge, where she extracted a pint of low fat milk; then she picked up a small, brown, ceramic sugar bowl from the counter. Placing both on the table, she sat down across from him, a steaming mug of coffee on the table in front of her.

"Aren't you going to eat?" he asked as he looked at her.

She shrugged. "I already did. While you were in the shower." Her every move sent familiar signals to his groin.

With her dark eyes and full breasts, Emily didn't need much more to make her memorable.

Grinning at her, he began to eat, quickly realizing he was hungrier than he'd thought. Consequently he made quick work of the food.

Silently she watched him while taking occasional sips from her steaming cup.

Just as he finished eating, the doorbell rang. Emily's smooth brow wrinkled, clearly annoyed at the disturbance of their quiet morning together. He frowned and started to get up from the table.

Stopping him with a wave her hand, Emily stood. "I'll get it," she said. "You finish your coffee."

He nodded. She disappeared and he heard the front door open.

He couldn't make out what they were saying, but he definitely heard a man's voice.

Suddenly the air was shattered with a high-pitched scream.

Bruce jumped up; the chair slammed to the floor as he ran for the front door. There in the open door was a cop. He was wearing those reflective sunglasses so you couldn't see his eyes. His pale brown uniform shirt bore a shiny silver star over the left breast pocket. Emily stood with her head buried in her hands, sobs wracking her body.

Stopping, he saw what was in the cop's right hand. His heart skipped a beat as recognition set in. He had seen it before. It was one of Sharon's red fuck-me high heels. The ones she had been wearing last night when she had collapsed in his arms. He realized right away what had happened.

Looks like I was wrong, Sharon didn't come home.

***

Bruce could see that Deputy Sheriff Kelly Summers was trying his best to be as diplomatic as possible under the circumstances.

"Where on the beach was the shoe found, Deputy?" asked Bruce. He hoped his gut was wrong this time, though when it came to Sharon, it had rarely been. Ever since they were kids growing up in King County near Seattle, he had always been closest to Sharon of all the members of his family. Being the baby of seven siblings, he had always looked up to Sharon as big sister and protector when they were kids.

As adults, now he was the one who often came to her rescue. Somehow, he'd always been there when she had needed him, like last night, he thought bitterly.

But this time he'd been too late to bail her out of whatever mess she'd gotten herself into.

"A man walking his dog on the beach found it early this morning. Above the high tide mark near the Inn at Spanish Head. But I'm afraid that doesn't make much difference. The winds were very strong last night and the surf was very high. Sneaker waves are particularly dangerous this time of year. We already lost six people this year to those damn things." Summers shook his head and the corners of his eyes sagged.

The deputy had taken off his sunglasses when he'd come inside. Bruce and he were seated on the couch together while Emily sat across from them in the stuffed chair, her eyes cast downward and tears still spilling slowly down her cheeks. Summers' badge had a high shine and his shirt had those crisp, pressed lines. His gold-plated nametag hung over his right shirt pocket and both pockets were securely buttoned.

In his lap was a black leather notebook, flipped open to a blank page. In neat script, he had written the date, the time, and their full names. Hatless, his blond hair was cut in a short military buzz cut like the good cop he appeared to be. His sunglasses hung by one arm from his left shirt pocket.

"Do you have any idea why she might've been on the beach last night?" asked the deputy.

Bruce experienced a flash of anger, not at Summers, but at himself. "I'm not my sister's keeper." He failed to hide the bitterness in his voice.

Summers shook his head. "No, of course not."

There was an awkward silence. "Is there anyone I should call?"

"Naw, I'll take care of it," said Bruce.

"What about her?" asked Summers, nodding toward Emily.

"She'll be all right. Won't you, Emily?" Bruce didn't use her nickname. He knew from experience that cops tended to home in on such details, thinking they had deeper meaning than just being a good-time girl.

Emily nodded silently, her eyes swollen from crying.

Summers rose from the couch and offered his hand to Bruce. Standing, Bruce took Summers hand in his and gave it a firm shake.

"I'd better be off, then. Sorry for your loss, Mr. Wilson."

Emily stayed where she was while Bruce followed the cop to the front door. Summers flipped open his sunglasses with practiced ease, placing them over his gray eyes. After his notebook was in his back pants pocket, he stepped onto the cement landing outside the front door.

"If you recall anything else, Mr. Wilson, please call me right way."

"Yeah, sure." Bruce said before he closed the door.

***

Summers hurried down the steps toward the white Pontiac patrol cruiser parked in the driveway. Standing beside the driver's door, he paused to survey the area. The sheriff always said he should be observant about his surroundings. Details solved cases, not clues you accidentally stumbled across. There was no luck in crime detection, just good cops being observant. Well, the sheriff had been acting strange lately kind of nervous for a cold as dead fish son of a bitch. And Summers had seen him several times with the dead girl in restaurants around town, and at a couple of the motels. A few times he'd seen her wearing shoes very like the one found on the beach. *Yeah, I'll show him I'm observant.*

It occurred to him it seemed odd a woman would wear high heels on a sandy beach at night but to each his own. She was probably dead, but somehow with Miller's involvement he didn't think it was an accident. Why should I give a shit? People go missing on the beach all the time. Another dead whore wasn't worth the trouble of confronting the sheriff.

Smiling briefly, he took in a lung full of salt air, then expelled it slowly. Today was a good day after all.

Opening the cruisers door, he stepped inside and slipped the key into the ignition. The powerful V-8 engine roared to life with a throaty growl. Shifting the car into gear after glancing over his shoulder, he stepped lightly on the gas pedal and backed the large, four-door patrol car out of the paved driveway onto the gravel road.

Once on the road, he shifted into drive and started to pull away. He glanced at the motorcycle on its steel kickstand as he passed. Bikers didn't impress him. They were all criminals as far as he was concerned. Too bad he's sniffing around Emily. She is sure cute, he thought. A woman like her needed a strong man like him in her life. An honest cop she could count on.

But Summers could see the biker and Emily were attracted to each other. I'm the observation king.

Maybe he'd ask her out after that stupid son of a bitch biker blew town. Shrugging, he drove the patrol car up the hill until he was over the crest, catching a final glimpse of the bungalow in the rear view mirror.

Eight

BRUCE STEERED HIS BIKE INTO AN EMPTY PARKING SPOT in front of
the Hair Club. The glowing red sign over the glass door reflected his
mood. He was numb from the seething knot of regret in his belly.
Sharon was probably dead. They'd been through a lot together over
the years, but too many people had dismissed her as some sultry
airhead. She was a person, damn it, and he loved her.

It was still early. The mall full of shops wouldn't open for
another hour, but he could see Trudy through the windows of
the hair shop, sweeping the floor with a wooden-handled broom.
The broom's blue plastic bristles were well worn. She swept like
someone on a mission to do damage. Her full brown curls hid her
eyes, her attention focused on the floor.

Bruce slipped off his helmet as he dismounted his motorcycle.
Kicking the stand in place, he dismounted then walked to the glass
door.

The door had one of those films on it to filter the sunlight. He
saw his reflection in the glass. He looked tired. His eyes had dark
circles under them and were bloodshot.

He tapped on the glass.

Trudy stopped sweeping and looked up. Seeing who it was, she frowned.

After resting the broom against a cutting chair, she walked to the door. She turned the deadbolt, swung the door open, then stood aside to let him in.

"Want some coffee?" she asked, her voice edged with heaviness. Her eyes said she wanted him to leave, but she was being polite.

"Sure."

Turning the deadbolt back to lock the door again, she turned and led him toward the office at the rear of the shop. On the way, she retrieved the broom.

Just inside the office doorway, she suddenly tossed the broom into the corner. "Fucking useless thing," she said spitting out the words.

"Why don't you buy a new one?" he asked.

When she turned to face him, he took a step back. Her eyes burned into him, her brow was creased with deep ridges. "Why don't you buy a new one?" she said before bursting into tears and burning her face in her hands.

Bruce put his arm around her shoulders and guided her into the office. Behind the veneer desk was a worn blue secretarial chair. He eased her into it.

Once seated, she sagged onto her crossed arms on the desk. The room smelled of coffee and perm solution.

Bruce fidgeted, watching her body wracked by heavy sobs. He wondered if this would forever be his role in life, to be a comfort to crying women.

"Listen," he said, "it's not that bad. Maybe Sharon'll be found and she'll be all right."

Her head popped up so fast it startled him. "Sharon? What about her?"

"She's missing. The cops think she's been swept away in the ocean. They think she was on the beach last night and a sneaker wave, whatever that is, got her."

"Good," she said as she swiped her eyes with the back of her right hand. Her eyes were swollen and puffy, but her face was already beginning to brighten.

His eyes narrowed. "What the hell are you so happy about? She's my sister."

Trudy went to the coffeemaker and poured them each a cup of the steaming brew. He nodded when she held up the sugar bowl, so she added two spoonfuls. He shook his head for the powered cream substitute.

Handing him a cup, she took her favorite green mug to the desk and gazed into his eyes. Earlier he'd spotted a small, pale orange stool with wheels underneath a metal storage rack that contained boxes of hairdresser supplies and laundry soap. Reaching underneath the rack, he rolled the stool across the tiled floor to sit across from her.

Trudy's brown eyes remained focused on Bruce as she reached for her black faux leather purse. After unzipping the bronze zipper, she reached inside. She withdrew a folded piece of white paper. She offered it to Bruce.

"What's this?" asked Bruce. Placing his black coffee cup on the desk, he accepted the paper from Trudy.

Unfolding it, he read the words, his mouth moving as he did. When he'd finished reading, his jaw tightened and a knot formed in his stomach. "Your husband?"

She nodded.

Bruce eased back in the chair. Trudy glared at him, her arms crossed over her chest. "Listen. I think we got off on the wrong foot here. I know my sister can be…"

"She's a slut and she's fired."

"I think she's dead." He surprised himself. Though he'd thought them, he hadn't actually said those words out loud until now. Sharon was always getting herself into scrapes, but somehow she always bounced back. This time felt different.

"Maybe she'd just busy fucking some other woman's husband."

Bruce's anger flared but he managed to suppress it. Trudy must be hurting. Sharon—and Trudy's husband—were to blame, not Trudy.

"Can I see her station?" he asked.

Trudy got up, leading the way into the shop. The black numbers and dashes on the white face of the clock hanging above the front door showed there was half an hour until the shop opened for business. On the plaza outside, the tourists' cars were starting to fill the lot. The coffee shops in the mall were open for business already; they attracted the early-riser crowd.

Sharon's station was covered with a gray towel upon which sat a collection of brushes and combs. In a hole in the station top was a hand-held hair dryer. A glass bottle with a silver lid sat at the back of the station in front of the mirror; it was filled with blue water.

He opened the drawer to discover a collection of notes and cards. There were the obligatory pennies and a makeup kit.

Leaving the pennies and the makeup kit untouched, he pulled out the stack of cards and notes. Underneath was a black notebook with gold lettering across the front. It read, in old-fashioned script, "My Little Black Book."

He cringed. This was his sister's private life, and it was awfully big for a little black book.

Setting the notes and cards in a pile on top of the combs and brushes, he cradled the black notebook in his left hand. Opening the book, he turned to the first page. There were lists of telephone numbers with only initials beside each one. Bruce recognized the phone numbers were from various towns around the state.

The book was tabbed and divided into various alphabetical categories. The first page was As and began with the initials BA. The number was an Oregon area code. It looked familiar for some reason.

"I need to take this with me, if that's okay with you?"

Trudy nodded. "You can take all her crap if you want it."

He nodded in kind. "Do you have a bag I can put this stuff in?"

Trudy disappeared into the office. She returned in a few moments carrying a white plastic garbage bag. He put everything—the combs, brushes, hairdryer and electric clippers that were hanging off the side of the station on a white plastic-coated hook, notes, cards, and the notebook—inside the bag.

"I'll be going now," he said. Trudy nodded and accompanied him to the front door. She unlocked it and held it open for him as he went outside.

Stopping, Bruce turned toward her before she closed the door. "Sorry."

Without responding, she closed the door and locked it. He watched her walk away without looking back until she disappeared into the office. The office door closed with a bang audible through the glass.

Bruce turned away and moved to stand beside his motorcycle. The air smelled of rain and the clouds overhead had grown darker. *Just like my life,* he thought.

After stowing the bag containing Sharon's stuff in the black, studded saddlebag that hung on the right side of the seat, he straddled his bike. Starting the engine, he gunned it a couple of times. The air filled with the odor of burnt oil and gasoline.

He slipped his skull helmet over his head, then pulled the strap tight under his chin. Next he used his feet to push the heavy bike backward out of the parking stall. As he turned the bike around, he had an elevated view of the parking lot. Parked near the main entrance of the mall, he saw a sheriff's department patrol car. Inside, a cop stared back at him.

Releasing the clutch as the bike started rolling, he weaved his way slowly through the growing rush of incoming bargain seekers. By the time he managed to get to the entrance of the mall, the white patrol car had disappeared.

His gut told him something wasn't right. He gunned the engine, then increased speed as he turned onto the main road. He needed to run Sharon's black book by Emily to see if she knew who these initials represented. His sister's death made no sense and he was determined to find out what had really happened.

Nine

ROCKY SQUINTED AS THE GUARD SLAPPED ON the overhead lights in the row of holding cells. The place reeked of urine and mice, and his head ached something fierce. His stomach heaved, but since he hadn't eating anything for at least a day, there was nothing to come up.

"Come on, fella," said the guard gruffly. The man's round, grinning face came into focus. His badge was so shiny it made Rocky's eyes hurt. "We gotta get you processed and released."

The cop—the brass nametag over his left shirt pocket said his name was Summers—selected a large steel key from the ring he had strapped to a silver key holder on his heavy black Sam Brown belt. He pulled it out like it was a fishing line, then plugged it in the lock on Rocky's cell door. When he turned the key, there was a metal-on-metal sound, causing Rocky to wince, then the cop swung the steel-bar door open.

Rocky pushed up from the thin gray blanket covering the lumpy mattress on the bunk and shielded his eyes with his right hand. In the opposite corner against the dirty brick wall was a stainless steel toilet.

"Do you have ta make all that noise?" Rocky asked. Rising on unsteady legs, he stumbled across the cell. His checkered sport coat reeked of stale booze and cigarettes. There were sweat stains under his armpits, and the gray stubble on his face had begun to itch. He scratched the tip of his pointed chin. His fringe of dark hair felt as if it were glued to his head, which, given the amount of gel he'd put in his hair yesterday, wasn't altogether surprising.

"Can I make a call?"

Summers laughed and slapped a hand on his shoulder. "You're not under arrest, pal, you don't get one phone call.

"You know sumthin, Wilson, you smell like cat pee."

Rocky smiled weakly and followed the chuckling cop into the front office through the door from the holding area. He held his pants over his bulging stomach with one hand. His belt was missing.

Summers nodded at his paunch. "Now don't you let those pants of yours slip. We got a lady out here and I'll have to arrest you for indecent exposure, understand?" Summers grinned.

The front office contained six ancient wooden desks, with phones and computers on them. The chairs were newer. They were the ergonomic kind, with rotating seats and three-wheeled tripods underneath the cloth seats. At one of the desks near the front of the room sat a woman talking on a telephone. She was speaking softly enough that he couldn't make out what she was saying. Slouched slightly forward, she had her back to him. She had dark hair. Her lithe frame was clothed in a gray suit jacket with matching slacks.

On the ride to the station she told Rocky her name was Detective Dolores Sanchez of the Oregon State Police and she said she had come along to observe Summers procedures.

Summers led Rocky to one of the desks and motioned for him to sit on the metal-framed black leatherette chair sitting next to it.

He did so, happy to be able to sit down again. The booze from last night still made him feel woozy.

The windows out front showed it was daytime now, but dark clouds still marred the view of the mountains. Hard rain had begun to fall; the wind was slamming large drops against the panes of glass, reminiscent of hail.

The desk drawer beside Summers scraped loudly and stuck halfway open. "Damn, we have to get these things waxed. Don't we, Sanchez?"

The woman turned, flipped him the middle finger salute, then returned to her telephone conversation. Summers chuckled.

Rocky realized why he couldn't understand what she was saying—she was speaking Spanish.

Summers applied additional force to the wooden drawer until, with a jerk and a creak, it finally slid the rest of the way out. Reaching in, he pulled out a green file folder. There was a white sticker on the top edge of the folder. Rocky's name was written in black ink on the sticker.

Rocky's heart rate increased. Why do I have a police file?

"I thought you would put me in the computer," said Rocky, nodding toward the monitor on the desk.

Summers smiled thinly. "Don't you worry, my friend. You'll be in there soon enough." Summers patted the monitor as if it was his favorite dog.

"Listen, all I was doing was having a few drinks…"

"And one of our patrols picked you up outside the Whaler, right?" asked Summers, his stern expression and serious dark eyes bored into Rocky.

Rocky squirmed beneath Summers intense gaze as if he were under hot lights. He wrung his hands. What had he done?

I like to drink. So what? That isn't a crime. Maybe I did something I don't remember?

"I really gotta make that call."

Summers glanced up at Sanchez, who was now looking back at them. She nodded. Summers said, "Okay. Use my phone."

Summers pushed the black, space-age looking phone toward him. It had a couple of phone numbers on the buttons that ran down one side and a little digital screen, which lit up when he lifted the receiver.

Rocky dialed his home number, but only got the answering machine. He decided not to leave a message. He needed a real person, not some machine. He cursed under his breath.

Summers eyes were focused on filling out the form; he made a circular motion with one finger to indicate he could keep dialing.

Next he dialed the Hair Club's number.

The line rang twice before Trudy's voice answered. She sounded tired.

"Good morning, Hair Club. How may I help you?"

Cupping his left hand around the receiver he whispered, "Trudy." Glancing at Summers, he was relieved to see him still concentrating on the form. Sanchez was still embroiled in her conversation.

"Rocky?"

"Yeah, listen, sweetie, I'm in a real jam and—" The line went dead. They had been cut off. He dialed the number again.

"Good morning…"

"Trudy, please don't hang up. I'm serious. I've been detained by the cops." He realized Summers was staring at him, shaking his head. He needed to gain her attention somehow.

There was a short pause on the other end of the line. "I'm listening," she said, her voice dry as the Mojave Desert.

"I was at the bar last night…"

"How unusual."

"Yeah… uh… I mean, no… I mean… well, anyway, I ran into this cop and he dragged me to jail. They thought I'd been drinking and driving, which I hadn't…"

"Like you never do that." Her voice dripped with sarcasm.

"Anyway, I think there's something else going on here and…" This time Summers had cut the connection by placing his fingers over the button in the receiver's cradle, disconnecting them.

"Hey, what gives?" Anger tightened Rocky's guts.

"Now you're being detained for questioning, asshole," said Summers.

Sanchez had turned her chair completely around. She was on her feet, moving toward him, dangling a pair of open handcuffs off her fingers. Over the breast pocket of her gray pantsuit hung a shiny gold badge with the words "State Police" and "Detective" prominently displayed. On one side of her wide hips, attached to her belt, was a leather holster containing an automatic pistol. The black butt of the gun stood out in contrast to the pure white of her thin blouse.

"What for?" asked Rocky as Detective Sanchez slipped first one then the other handcuff around his wrists and locked them.

"We're investigating the murder of Sharon Carstairs, and you're a person of extreme interest" said the raven-haired Sanchez, her face grim, her dark eyes determined.

Rocky's breath caught in his throat. *Sharon? Dead?*

Ten

WHEN THE CALL WAS INTERRUPTED, Trudy hung up, slowly returning the receiver to the cradle. Mrs. Armstrong called to her, waking her as if from a dream. Mrs. Armstrong was under the hair dryer and the buzzer had sounded to indicate she was done.

Maybe Rocky was really in trouble this time? He may be a cheating son of a bitch, but he was still her husband.

She hurried to help Mrs. Armstrong. The look on her face must've startled the old woman.

"Is something wrong, dear?" The older woman's eyes were curious. The old ladies in this town loved gossip nearly as much as they loved the tabloids she kept in the shop for them to read. Mrs. Armstrong had been reading the most current tabloid as she sat beneath the dryer.

Trudy forced her mouth into a smile, but her eyes remained vacant and preoccupied as she considered her next move. She had to get to the police station as soon as possible, but there were other appointments on the book for today. She'd call them after Mrs. Armstrong left and arrange appointments for another day. She might lose customers, but that was how it must be.

For the first time in a long time, her husband needed her.

"Family comes first," her father always said.

"For better or worse," her mother added when she'd first laid eyes on Rocky.

God, how I hate clichés... they always come back to haunt you.

"Okay, Mrs. Armstrong, let's see how beautiful you look today, shall we?"

Mrs. Armstrong smiled at the compliment. Her gray skin and wrinkled complexion had once been young and fresh. Now she looked like an old potato sack.

Trudy pulled back the dryer cover and started removing the rollers.

***

An hour after the call from Rocky, Trudy arrived at the Fairview police station. She parked the Chevette in an empty stall near the front doors.

Stepping out of the car, she held her navy nylon coat over her head as a shield from the raindrops.

She managed to get to the front doors without getting too wet. She stepped inside after opening the door; the bell over the door tinkled brightly announcing her.

A cop, in the traditional uniform of brown pants with a chocolate colored stripe down the side and tan, short-sleeved shirt, sat behind a desk reading a magazine. Trudy saw it was a gun magazine. She smirked. A cop obsessed with guns? How clichéd can you get?

Looking at her over the top of his magazine, the cop sighed and dropped the open magazine on the desk in front of him.

The fluorescent lights added brightness to the chipped paint on the walls behind him. The blinds on the front windows were open. The office smelled of donuts and coffee.

"Can I help you?" The cop leaned on his elbows, his pale face expressionless and his blond hair neatly combed with a perfect part. He wore no tie and his white undershirt was visible through the open collar of his uniform shirt. The silver badge over his left shirt pocket gleamed.

Picking up a blue plastic ballpoint pen, he began to click it. Obviously a nervous habit.

"Yes," she said. The cop's arrogance was already beginning to wear thin with her. "I understand you're holding Rocky Wilson here."

"Yup. And who are you?" he grinned sardonically, his eyes twinkling.

"I'm his wife." Holding up her chin, she returned his steady gaze.

"You better have a seat." Standing, he waved a hand at the wooden office chair near the door. She sensed his sudden uneasiness. She watched him pick up the phone receiver on his desk, then push a single button.

Trudy heard what sounded like a feminine voice answer. "You better come out here." There was a short pause while the muffled voice of the woman said something she couldn't make out. "His wife's here, that's why."

He replaced the receiver.

"Has something happened to my husband?" asked Trudy.

"Detective Sanchez will explain. She's on her way out."

Trudy shrugged and folded her hands across her lap. The cop eyed her silently. His eyes kept drifting toward a closed door to his left, then back to her.

Trudy was about to insist on answers when the door swung open. A Hispanic woman with shoulder-length dark hair and deep red lips, wearing a gray pantsuit with a thin white blouse visible beneath, walked into the room.

She wasn't heavy, just full figured, and her expression suggested someone who knew her business. The polished gold badge sticking from her suit's breast pocket was attached to a leather wallet and glinted in the artificial lighting.

As she approached, her expression changed to a white, toothy smile and her face seemed to soften. Trudy thought this woman should smile more often, but being a cop, and a detective at that, probably meant she didn't have many opportunities to smile. No, being a cop was serious business.

The detective held out her right hand, which Trudy grasped in kind. "Hello, Mrs. Wilson. I'm Detective Sanchez of the Oregon State Police Criminal Investigation Unit."

Trudy's heart skipped a beat. Didn't CIU investigate murders? Was Rocky dead?

Sanchez placed a hand around Trudy's shoulder. "Why don't we talk in the back?" With her other hand, Sanchez motioned toward the open door.

Trudy nodded, too stunned to say anything. What had Rocky been up to? Her mind swirled with darker and darker scenarios.

Sanchez guided Trudy to the interrogation room past three private offices. The detective caught Summers' eye as they passed his desk. He nodded, then eased himself down in his chair.

"Summers, we'll be in the back," Sanchez explained. "Girl talk, you know how it is?" One corner of her mouth curled up in a half smile.

They passed the cell holding Rocky; he sat on the bunk, shoulders slumped, his face flushed crimson. His complexion could be embarrassment, or booze, or both. A mix of anger and relief that he was alive washed over Trudy. What was really going on here, and why was Rocky in a cell? Had he been arrested? And if so, then what had he done? She hoped Detective Sanchez had some answers for her.

At the interrogation room, Sanchez opened the door and ushered her inside. The room contained two wooden office chairs, sitting on either side of a plain wooden table. The table's varnish peeled in places and there was nothing on it. The fluorescent lights illuminated the room in a soft glow.

Sanchez offered her a chair with the wave of one hand. After Trudy sat down, Sanchez turned the other chair around so the back faced Trudy. Sanchez straddled the chair, resting her arms across the top of the chair back.

The sheriff's station had been built in the fifties, at a time when cops were a little rougher around the edges than the college grads recruited by most departments today. Trudy doubted the interrogation room had changed since the station was built, since the room reeked of tobacco smoke, mingled with the faint odor of mold.

Sanchez's brown eyes stared at Trudy, her expression noncommittal.

"Do you know why we detained your husband?"

"Drunk driving?"

Sanchez shook her head. "No. We think your husband was involved in Sharon Carstairs' disappearance. We suspect her death was no accident," she added, being more pointed.

Trudy's eyes grew wide. "You think she was murdered?"

Sanchez frowned. "We don't know what to think, but the evidence we've gathered thus far seems to lean toward foul play. The deputy found a red shoe above the tideline. Her brother says it's Sharon's.

"At first, we thought her disappearance might be accidental. She was on the beach during a storm, after all, and quite a few unwary types are lost to the ocean every year." Sanchez shrugged. "Nothing unusual about that. But given Sharon's..." Her words trailed off and she arched an eyebrow.

Trudy lowered her chin to her chest and closed her eyes. Opening her eyes, she looked at the detective with what she hoped was the most sincere expression she could muster. "Is there anything I can do to help?" she asked.

Sanchez gave her a thin smile. "Do you know where your husband was last night?"

Anger rose from Trudy's belly at the mention of Rocky's whereabouts. It quickly passed and she hoped her feelings weren't on display. Rocky's a son of a bitch and a pain in the ass, but he isn't a killer. If anything, he's a coward.

"I thought he was at the Whaler, like he usually is."

"And you. Where were you?" Sanchez's dark eyes narrowed.

Trudy eyed the detective, her brow wrinkled. It dawned on her what was happening. "You think I was involved in Sharon's death, don't you?" The anger, frustration, and sense of betrayal spilled out of her at Sanchez. The detective crossed her arms, saying nothing, her expression placid. Trudy jumped up, shoving the chair back from the table with sufficient force it fell backward, landing with a thud on the floor.

"How dare you! If you want to say any more, then you better arrest me."

Sanchez made no move to retrieve her handcuffs or stand up. She sat impassively, watching Trudy.

"I'm outta here."

Trudy spun around and was out the door and into the hallway before Sanchez could stop her. The little brass lock rattled as she slammed the door shut behind her. Before leaving, she stopped and glared at Rocky in his cell. He kept his eyes focused on the floor.

She spat, then hurried down to end of the corridor and through the office. Once outside the station and inside her car, Trudy took in a deep, but shaky, breath. For a few seconds she drew in deep breaths to steady her pounding heart and ease her trembling hands. She hadn't given a performance like that since her high school days.

Chuckling, she started the Chevette's engine. A trail of blue smoke followed her onto the highway as she left the sheriff's station behind.

Eleven

DOLORES SANCHEZ OPENED THE MANILA FOLDER to study the few
pieces of paper in the file. The pretty brunette, olive-skinned,
Hispanic detective suspected she was wasting her time. She eyed
Summers, who had his feet on top of his desk and was reading a
comic book. He was chewing his gum loudly, stopping every few
minutes to snap it between his teeth. She could smell the too-sweet
gum. These small-town cops were virtually useless except to direct
traffic or write parking tickets. This guy in particular was a real piece
of work.

Sanchez was actually in Fairview on a clandestine investigation
due to rumors at the State capital of corruption within the local
sheriff's office. Her commanding officer had been adamant she
keep her true assignment from the locals. A convenient murder
investigation meant she wouldn't have to use the lame cover story
that she was here to audit the sheriff's procedures. A CIU detective
auditing would seem odd but she would try to explain it away as
the result of state budget restraints. She didn't even believe it when
the captain explained it to her so she'd have to do one hell of an
acting job to sell it. But for now she could assist with the murder
investigation, if there really was a murder.

Rolling her eyes, she returned to reading the information in the file. At least the town sheriff was a pretty good cop. Sheriff John Miller was originally from the Portland PD. She understood he'd left Portland after twenty years on the force. He said he liked the quiet of small-town life. But rousting a few kids during spring break or dealing with a few domestic disputes seemed pretty dull work for a former homicide cop.

Homicide tended to jade your perception of the world, and even though she had only been in the state police homicide division for two years, she found herself already becoming the ultimate cynic about human nature. The things human beings would do to each other for the smallest rewards continued to amaze her.

The file said Sharon Carstairs had last been seen by her two roommates two nights ago, leaving her house. Sanchez already interviewed them and confirmed the initial reports.

Emily had been a little evasive in her responses. Obviously, she didn't trust cops. Her statement was suspect at best, an outright lie at worst. The other roommate, Alice, wasn't too bright. She'd been a deer in the headlights when she'd found out Sharon was missing and presumed dead.

Rocky Wilson—there was an interesting suspect. Loser with a drinking problem, and evidently a skirt chaser. He and the vic had been cozy, something his wife hadn't known about. Maybe Trudy Wilson had found out and had taken the law into her own hands? A woman scorned? Such things had happened before and would happen again. Rocky had been released already because they didn't have enough evidence to hold him, but maybe putting the two suspects together would make one of them crack.

Rocky had a lot to lose if Sharon told his wife about his nocturnal activities.

Not only the marriage, but also the business, the house, everything. When you dip your wick, you have to pay the price sooner or later. Sanchez shrugged.

No matter who was right or wrong, one of them probably did it. Her problem was the evidence was mostly circumstantial. Sharon's collection of answering machine tapes had a few interesting tidbits on them. She'd sent the tapes to the crime lab in Portland shortly after she'd found them at the house. Those tapes and the one red shoe, which Emily had identified as being Sharon's, were the two key factors that led Miller to suspect foul play. She hadn't revealed everything she had to the chief suspects yet, just enough to coax them along. Something would break loose soon.

Sighing, she closed the file folder. She pushed back the wooden chair where she sat. This entire office was right out of the fifties. What a dump, she thought.

Summers dropped his feet to the floor. "Is there something I can help you with?" he asked, a look of coyness on his pale face.

"I'm going back to the Overlook," she said.

The motel was a real dump, but there weren't many choices of accommodation in this town. Especially when she was forced to travel on a meager stipend. The captain would be really pissed if she blew the budget on nice digs.

"Wanta have coffee later?" asked Summers, really looking pathetic now. Was the son of a bitch kidding, or what?

"Not in this lifetime, Summers."

She stood and walked from behind the desk, feeling his eyes following her. It made her skin crawl when he watched her. Her open suit jacket flapped against her side as she walked. Her dark, shoulder-length hair bounded against her shoulders as she headed for the door to the parking lot.

Exiting out the front door, she took in a lungful of fresh, salt air and smiled to herself. A light breeze had sprung up now and the clouds had parted, letting a little blue sky appear and rays of golden sunshine fall on her face. Maybe small-town life was the way to go; maybe Sheriff Miller had the right idea.

Pulling out her car keys, she opened the door to her white Ford four-door. After climbing inside, she started the engine, then paused to think.

No, she wasn't going back to the motel. She had something to check out first. She drove off, leaving a trail of wispy exhaust behind her.

***

Summers had moved to the window, holding up one blind, watching Sanchez through narrow eyes until she drove away. Dropping the dusty blind, he wiped his hands on his uniform pant legs. He grunted, ambled back to the desk, and went back to reading his comic book.

Twelve

TRUDY PARKED WHERE THE PAVEMENT ENDED, looking out over miles of gray, sandy beach. Bruce's motorcycle sat resting on its stand; beads of rainwater covered the purple gas tank and dripped off the chrome pipes that ran down the side of the massive bike. She could see that the waves across the horizon were light now, but the sky boiled with alternating light and dark clouds, as if an unseen war was going on in the sky.

The town had buried a yellow, diamond-shaped sign on a steel post in the brown earth where the pavement ended. The sign screamed "WARNING!" in large, block letters with a couple of small-font paragraphs beneath that she couldn't quite read. Probably some shit about watch out for high surf. A little late for Sharon.

Opening the car door, she was immediately swamped by the sour, salt odor of the ocean. A scattered flock of gray-and-white gulls rode the wind overhead on extended wings, emitting shrill cries that competed with the noises of the wind and the waves, pounding the shoreline.

The cold made her shiver.

She shoved her hands into the pockets of the heavy wool sweater she kept it in the car in case it got cold. The wool was rough and cold against her skin. Thankfully, it had stopped raining.

Walking to the front of the car, she spotted the sandy path leading onto the beach. There was a rough trail stamped down in the yellowed shore grass that she could follow.

She walked down the path onto the beach, then stood watching the green, foam-topped waves. Bruce was here somewhere. To her right was gray sand as far as she could see. There were only a few people in that direction, though from the shape of them, she could tell none of them was Bruce. Far too conservative, or far too female.

To her left, black volcanic rocks jutted from the sand like knife-edged mountains of coal. She stepped carefully in the sticky sand, her white runners sinking deeper with every step. It was more like walking across snow than wet sand.

Pulling her sweater tighter to shield her from the cold wind, she lowered her head and started trudging toward the nearest outcropping of black rock.

The tide was out so she could get around to the seaward side of the rock without being threatened by the waves.

Once around the other side, she found Bruce, sitting alone on the edge of the rocks, staring toward the horizon.

"Hey, Bruce!" she shouted, but the wind and pounding surf swallowed her voice. He didn't look in her direction.

Stepping carefully over the jagged rocks, she made her way toward him.

As she approached, her shadow fell over him and he finally glanced in her direction. His large blue eyes were red rimmed and the sadness in them made her stop walking. For a long moment, they stared at each other, not speaking.

Finally, he indicated she should sit on the relatively flat rock beside him.

She gingerly picked her way toward him and sat down. After sitting, she joined him, staring at the ocean, watching the waves. She realized for the first time since moving to Fairview that a sneaker wave could come out of nowhere at any time. The ocean was as unpredictable as the weather on the coast.

She noted a black nylon waterproof bag sitting between Bruce's feet on the rock.

"What's in there?" she asked, raising her voice in order to be heard above the din.

He shrugged. "Notes, letters, and a book. Junk, really." He tossed the bag onto the sand a few feet away from the rock and watched as the waves rushed to carry it away as the ocean had done with his sister.

"Yours?" she asked, not meaning to pry but to make conversation.

"Naw, Sharon's stuff. You know, the stuff from the shop."

Trudy watched as a larger wave rush toward the bag. It failed to reach it, but the tide was turning and soon enough the surf would swallow the bag and its contents. Sharon's memories and all she had been could soon disappear forever...

Trudy frowned. "Cards? Letters? A book?" she asked softly. "Oh, my…" Leaping to her feet, she scrambled down the rocks to the sand, almost falling as she ran. Seeing that the waves were getting closer to the bag, she dove across the sand and grabbed it. She rolled over and came up with the bag before the waves could take it out to sea.

When she looked up, Bruce's bulk stood over her, his large shadow falling across her face.

His expression was a mixture of surprise and confusion.

"This bag may contain clues about what really happened to Sharon," she gasped, breathing hard from the sudden exertion.

Bruce stared at her. "You are one crazy bitch. Sharon's dead. The cops told me it was an accident."

"Then why would they want to hold Rocky and me on suspicion of murder?" Trudy realized she'd made a mistake the moment the words were out of her mouth.

Bruce's brow furrowed, then his cheeks grew crimson and his eyes narrowed, his mouth formed a grim line, then anger. "You killed her?" he asked between gritted teeth.

Oh, crap. "Of course not," she said, rising to her knees, clutching the bag in her right hand. With her other hand, she balanced herself on the sand. Standing, she brushed the wet sand off her jeans and jacket. Sand had a way of getting into every nook and cranny where it would stubbornly refuse to leave.

Bruce eyed her suspiciously but made no move toward her. "What? I don't get it."

"Neither do I, yet. But I think the contents of this bag will tell us more. I think she was murdered." She scanned the mostly deserted beach. The light was beginning to fade as the clouds darkened overhead, the surf becoming gradually higher with each passing moment.

Bruce scowled. "Why would you say that?"

Trudy shook her head. "Oh, it wasn't me. It was that cop, Sanchez. She said she thought someone killed Sharon."

"Come on, Trudy, cops say all kinds of shit to get a reaction."

"But why would she want a reaction from me? Maybe I'm a suspect?"

Bruce looked at her in silence until his eyes narrowed. "Did you kill my sister?"

"Of course not, but if we check out this bag, we may find a clue to the identity of the real killer."

Bruce snorted. "Then why don't we give the bag to that lady cop?"

Trudy felt her cheeks grow warm. "I put on a little performance for her. I don't think she's gonna want to talk to me for a while."

One corner of Bruce's mouth curled up. "I'm thinking I like you, Trudy Wilson."

She smiled.

"Wanta go to the Hilltop and get a cup of coffee? I think it's going to get real nasty here in a minute," Trudy suggested.

Bruce nodded and together they wove their way around the rocks and then across the open beach. Trudy's guts were knotted by fear. This biker could snap her neck with his strong hands and toss her into the sea, where no one would ever find her body.

Trudy knew she couldn't do this alone. She and Sharon's brother would have to team up if she was going to save her marriage, her business, and most importantly, her freedom. The bonus would be finding out what happened to Sharon.

Though she didn't know him well, her heart ached for Bruce. She could tell he loved his sister. Her compassionate nature tugged at her. But her husband and that tramp had...

She shook off the feelings of jealousy and anger. No, this was about more than her unfaithful husband, much more.

**

Since he'd walked to the beach from the motel, Trudy offered to drive Bruce to the Overlook Motel parking lot, where he had parked his bike. He'd explained that he'd walked the beach needing alone time to think.

He opened the passenger door to the scraping sound of rusted metal hinges. "Are you sure this piece of shit is safe?" He wrinkled his nose. The odor from inside the Chevette was of perfume and old makeup.

Casting him a withering look, she opened the driver's door, then slid behind the wheel. "Will you get in, please?" she asked, her tone impatient.

Bruce shrugged and attempted to sit on the stained plaid cloth seat, but his head struck the door frame. He uttered a string of words, some of which she'd never heard before. The car wasn't designed for guys his size.

"Ow." Rubbing the sore spot with the fingers of one hand, he managed to duck low enough to get in without further injuring himself. His knees were pressed against the dashboard and it looked like he might get hurled through the windshield if she had to stop quickly.

"The handle to move the seat back is underneath," said Trudy.

He nodded and tried to feel around beneath the seat to find it. He snorted, got out, bent over, and felt around until he located the handle, then pulled it up and pushed the seat back. Once it was as far back as it would go, he released the handle and was rewarded with a satisfying click as it locked into place.

Trudy grinned.

Smirking, he got back in the little car and again hit his head on the door frame. "For fuck's sake, ow!"

"Don't worry," said Trudy, "you'll get it eventually."

She started the engine; it ticked loudly as it came to life. The little car shuddered when she put it into gear. She glanced in the rearview mirror; the car shook around them as she gave it some gas and backed up.

Bruce gave her a worried look as he pulled the tan-colored seatbelt across his bulky frame. It wasn't long enough, so he released it and it snapped back. "Jeez, I hope some cop doesn't pull us over," Bruce said.

In most circumstances, Trudy would've laughed at his comment, but the situation had become too weird to be funny. Her sense of humor had disappeared. Instead of laughing, she smiled weakly and concentrated on the road ahead. They were soon at the junction of the side road and Highway 101. The traffic was heavy, so they'd have wait for an opening.

"How did you find me?" asked Bruce as the car pumped out a steady stream of white exhaust like a private, self-generated fog. The air inside the car was rank with the smell of burnt gasoline.

"I dropped by the house. Emily said I'd find you at the beach. I didn't know where exactly, but I searched until I found you," said Trudy, glancing both ways, looking for her opening in the rush of cars and trucks. "You are rather hard to miss.

"Ah," she said, "here we go." She gunned the little engine and turned as a space appeared. They joined the line of cars headed north.

A light rain had begun to fall so Trudy turned on the windshield wipers. They were small and clearly in need of replacement since they did little to clear the excess moisture from the windshield.

Tall evergreens lined the highway and they passed various tourist souvenir shops and restaurants as they drove.

Some had wooden clapboard signs out front advertising fresh seafood, and one advertised the best ribs on the Oregon coast. Bruce's stomach grumbled loudly.

Trudy glanced at him and smiled. He probably hadn't eaten much lately. "How's the food at the Hilltop?" he asked. "I've never been there."

Trudy shrugged. "Not bad."

In silence, Bruce stared out the passenger window at the passing trees.

"So, why were you going to throw away those notes and things?" asked Trudy, changing the subject. She kept her eyes focused on the car ahead of them.

"I dunno. My sis kept everything her boyfriends ever gave her. She said it was just in case." Trudy's gut tightened. Blackmail most likely. "I just wanted to get rid of that shit before…" His words choked off and his eyes filled with tears. "I miss her so much," he finally managed to whisper.

With her right hand, Trudy patted his knee and they continued in silence.

Trudy made the right turn into the parking lot of the Hilltop Family Restaurant. The large white sign with red lettering sat atop the steel post and was visible in both directions. It was a local hang out. A reasonably priced restaurant and not one the tourists tended to gravitate toward. Not flashy enough for the big city folks. Perfect for Trudy and Bruce.

"You up for some food in addition to the coffee?"

Bruce muttered his agreement.

Once parked, they got out; this time Bruce managed to get out with his head untouched. They walked side by side toward the glass front door of the restaurant.

They could see through the windows that the place was mostly deserted. A few blue hairs were scattered at various tables and there was one waitress. A man wearing a name badge and a cheap-looking green-and-white striped tie was moving about, clearing tables and making sure the few customers inside were happy.

A middle-aged couple sat at a table away from the seniors. He wore a black cowboy hat with a multicolored headband, and a gray goatee adorned his chin. The woman had shoulder-length gray hair pulled back with a hair band, and wire-rimmed glasses sat perched on her nose. They were having an animated conversation about something that appeared to be very important to both of them, evidenced by their heated debate.

Behind the pass bar into the kitchen, there were two Hispanic cooks wearing white uniforms and tall, white, paper chef's hats.

Coming into the restaurant were two sets of glass doors to pass through; the first contained a rubber grate to catch water and sand or dirt from people's shoes. Next to the doors was a cigarette machine. Trudy thought about buying a pack of smokes. She hadn't smoked in eight years, but the urge to take up her old bad habits had been growing the past few days. With recent events, she didn't know how long she could hold the dirty habit at bay.

Bruce held the first door for Trudy; she walked through and did likewise, holding the second door for him as they entered the restaurant's waiting area.

A brown wood sign with raised yellow lettering read, "Please Wait to be Seated." Trudy watched Bruce fidget until the manager, his belly straining the buttons on his plain white dress shirt, came over to greet them with his best "can I help you" smile. Trudy smiled thinly and held up two fingers to indicate the number of people in their party.

The slicked-down hair of the manager gleamed in the daylight coming through the windows. The man pulled two plastic-coated menus from a wooden slot attached to the side of the cash station.

"Come this way," he said.

Trudy and Bruce followed behind the manager, his cheap aftershave washing over them, souring Trudy's stomach. He led them toward the right side of the restaurant's seating area, away from the blue hairs. She was thankful for small mercies. She didn't want to run into any of her regular customers. They were bound to ask foolish questions concerning Sharon, which she didn't feel like answering right now.

No doubt word had spread around town, though the local weekly newspaper's reporter hadn't been around asking about the missing hairdresser on the beach. The local scandal sheet had been preoccupied with the kickback scandal involving the town elders for weeks now. One missing woman woujldn't be making headlines. Lots of people went missing every year on that beach. But how could they be so cold?

Trudy's eyes fixed on the back of Bruce's leather vest and his slumped shoulders as he walked ahead of her. Pain seemed to emanate from him in waves. Trudy shivered. He must be hurting, badly.

At the booth, they sat down and immediately Trudy ordered some tea while Bruce requested a coke. No ice.

The manager thanked them, then disappeared to get their drink order.

"What did you mean when you said you thought Sharon was murdered?" Bruce asked once they were alone. His eyes had grown hard and she could see his shoulders rise with tension as he asked the question.

90

"I don't believe her disappearing from that beach was an accident, that's all," Trudy said in a low voice. "The detecive told me the deputy found a red woman's shoe on the beach above the tideline and she said you confirmed it was Sharon's."

Bruce knitted his fingers together on the table in front of him.

"How many of Sharon's shoes did the cop show you?"

Bruce's brow wrinkled in thought before answering, "One. I think."

"Why only one? I don't understand how any woman walking on that beach would be wearing high heels. If she took them off voluntarily, then why didn't the cops have both of them? And if one was found above the high tide mark, then there should have been two, don't you think?"

Bruce's eyes became curious. "But maybe one was swept away by a sneaker wave like Sharon. Then there would only have been one."

Before Trudy could add anything more, the manager reappeared, carrying a black plastic tray with a cork surface holding a coffee cup, a stainless steel teapot, and a glass of cola. He set the tray on the table, placed Trudy's teapot and cup down in front of her—the smell of the orange pekoe filling the air—and the glass of bubbling cola in front of Bruce.

Trudy ordered some whole-wheat toast, Bruce a cheese sandwich and soup of the day. He didn't care what it was, just that it was hot. The manager wrote down their orders on the pad, then disappeared, carrying the tray toward the kitchen.

Trudy brought Bruce's bag, which she had kept between her legs underneath her chair until now, up onto the table. Beach sand still clung to the outside.

Checking first, to make sure no one was watching, she shook off the excess grains onto the carpeted floor, then brushed off any grains remaining on the table before placing the bag back in front of her.

"Let's take a look, shall we?" Trudy said.

Pulling the folded papers and thin cardboard cards from the bag, she stacked them in a jumbled pile since they weren't of uniform size. The book had worked its way to the bottom of the bag, so she removed it last, then tossed the empty bag again onto the floor between her legs.

Next, she separated the notes from the cards. She decided to look at the cards first. Her hands trembled as she lifted the first card off the pile. Fear gripped her. Maybe she was about to find out things about her husband she didn't want to know.

"Well?" asked Bruce as he leaned forward. She glanced at him. His face was flushed and his eyes expectant. Somehow it comforted her to think he was as nervous about this as she felt.

She opened the card on top of the pile, the one with a large red heart across it. The words "I WILL LOVE YOU FOREVER" were written in stylized red letters. Opening the card, she found the usual poetic wording and a number of x's and o's. Written in blue ink were the words, "FOR LAST NIGHT AND ALWAYS." Beneath that was a signature of someone named Ron.

Trudy fought the urge to laugh. Men were sure dummies when they thought with the lump of flesh between their legs.

The remaining cards were in a similar vein and it took until their food arrived for them to go through the stack of thirty. Bruce and she shared cards between them; they read each one carefully, looking for a pattern. All they found was that each card had a different guy's name inside. First names only. The cards weren't going to be much help.

They ate in silence. Trudy watched Bruce eat as she slowly chewed a corner of her toast. Bruce inhaled his sandwich. He was obviously starving. After finishing the last bite of crust on the sandwich, he sat back in the booth with a satisfied sigh. He seemed all right, for a biker.

"You're not a Hell's Angel or something, are you?" she asked, breaking the silence.

When he looked at her, his eyes twinkled and one corner of his generous mouth curled upward. "Why would you ask that?"

"I don't know. Something tells me this look of yours is a front." She crossed her arms over her chest and her brow wrinkled as she made eye contact with him.

He smiled, his white teeth showing. "You got me. Actually, I'm a bookkeeper for a motorcycle dealer in Seattle." He held the sides of his leather vest open with his long, meaty fingers. "These duds are for show. You have to wear the clothes and walk the talk if you want real bikers to trust you. The owners of the shop are bikers. They would never have hired me if they thought I was some kinda L7, and I needed the job." He shrugged. "Gotta eat." He patted his stomach to emphasis his point.

Trudy smiled.

"They nicknamed me Rice Burner. My bike isn't a Harley," he explained.

Trudy pictured Bruce's motorcycle in her mind. It had a fancy paint job. The name of the manufacturer was in raised silver letters across the side of the gas tank. Kawasaki. A Japanese company.

"Your bike is Japanese?"

"Yeah," he chuckled. "I love that bike. I restored it myself, long before I started at the shop.

"Real bikers say the only good motorcycle is a Harley Davidson, and they've been on my case to buy a Harley since I started working there five years ago." He shook his head. "But no way am I giving up my baby. Harley's are good, but my ride is better."

Trudy often wondered why people got so attached to inanimate objects. She thought of her Chevette. Sure it was a POS, but it got her where she wanted to go and that's what any transportation is supposed to do. *Must be a guy thing,* she concluded.

"You know, I could fix your car if you wanted me to. You pay for the parts and I'll do the work. Free of charge," offered Bruce.

Trudy looked indignant. "There's nothing wrong with my car."

"Actually, the electronic pickup sensor is going. That's why it runs so rough when the engine's cold."

She leaned toward him. "I hate to tell you this, Bruce, but it's a car, not a truck."

He grinned. "No, no, the electronic pickup. It's a device in your car that—"

She cut him off. "Never mind. We have better things to worry about right now." She hated it when people picked on her car. It was the only thing she truly owned, and very likely all she would have left after the business went under.

Bruce raised his hands in mock surrender. "Okay. okay. Sorry."

The manager reappeared. "Will there be anything else?" he asked.

"Yes, I'd like some more hot water and he'd like another coke," Trudy said, nodding toward Bruce.

"Of course," he said. He pocketed what must have been the bill and disappeared behind the short wall.

"Let's start going through these notes," Trudy said, wanting to divert the discussion to anything but her car.

Bruce nodded as the manager returned carrying a glass of cola and a glass urn filled with steaming water. He refilled Trudy's teapot and laid the bill face down on the table.

"That'll be all," said Trudy. "We don't want to be disturbed."

The manager nodded, picked up their dirty plates, and left them alone.

"I don't think he likes you much," Bruce said when the manager was out of earshot.

"He's a slimy son of a bitch. Boozes it up with my husband at the Whaler."

They started going through the stack of notes. They were much the same as the cards in that they contained expressions of undying love and devotion. A few had offers of marriage, while others were sleazy references to sexual trysts. The names were all different, but none appeared to be written by Rocky. A few had names like Hun Buns—someone couldn't spell—or Love Muffin, so those might have been from him, except he'd never accept terms of endearment like that, at least not that she'd ever heard.

Rocky always had a larger-than-life ego and he liked the sound of his name whenever the opportunity arose to say it out loud. He thought it sounded more like a real man's name, as if he were a tough guy or something. His real name was Harold, but he'd been using the Rocky nickname since high school. It probably had something to do with the first Rocky movie, but he claimed the Stallone character had nothing to do with his name.

The real tough guys in school would have kicked his ass if he claimed to be as tough as the movie Rocky. Her Rocky was far too much of a coward. She smirked and Bruce looked at her with a frown wrinkling his forehead.

"Nothing."

He nodded, then went back to reading the note in his hand.

After they had finished reviewing the notes, Trudy felt like she needed a long hot shower. Even then, the water probably wouldn't get rid of the overpowering smell of drugstore perfume.

"Well, I don't see anything in these that's going to help us," she said. "All we know now is that Sharon had a lot of male admirers."

Bruce nodded grimly. "Yeah, and knowing my sister, she probably played them all, too."

Sharon gave him a curious look. "Played them?"

"Yeah," he said with a sigh. "She collected men who could do her some good. Either financially or otherwise. She used sex to manipulate men. Her favorite saying was 'Sharon does what Sharon wants, when Sharon wants to.' The men's needs were not important." He shook his head sadly. "It looks like she used the wrong man and pushed him too far this time."

"Has she ever gone too far before?"

He nodded. "Yeah, she came close a few times. One guy in Seattle beat her up pretty bad. I took care of it." She opened her mouth to speak, but he held one meaty hand up to stop her. "You don't wanna know."

"Any others?" she asked.

"Yeah. She called me from Newport once and asked me ta come down there, said this guy was being a real pain. By the time I got time off and got there, she said the guy had disappeared and the problem was solved."

"How long ago was that?"

He shrugged. "I dunno. Maybe a year. Maybe a little more."

"Newport isn't very far from here. Maybe we should check the place out." She paused in thought. "Do you remember which hair shop she worked at there?"

He shook his head in wonderment. "Boy, Trudy, you're really some kinda detective."

She smiled thinly. He's so full of shit. He was playing dumb biker guy on purpose. She was sure she would find out why later.

"All right, let's see the book."

He pulled it from the bag and set it, still closed, on the table between them. Trudy spun it around to face her. In gold letters across the front were the words, "My Little Black Book." The thing was the size of the Fairview phone book.

She opened to the first page. There were little white alphabetical tags along the sides of some of the pages to divide them into various sections. In black uppercase letters, they started at A and ran to Z. Some sections were further divided to accommodate a greater number of names.

Trudy noted immediately that there were phone numbers and some addresses, though no names—just initials or some names that were obviously not real names, like Asshole, or when she flipped to the first page of S, Superman.

Trudy paused and stared at the W tag. With trembling fingers, she turned to that page and saw that there were no initials for RW. No Rocky Wilson, and Trudy's name wasn't in the book.

"Try the Rs," suggested Bruce.

Turning the pages of the book to the Rs, there were three groups of initials on the page. RR, RG and RS, but no Rocky. How could that be? Had he been a code word somewhere else in the book? Could he be the asshole? She wanted to believe he was the asshole, but he did have some good qualities, otherwise she never would have married him.

She slammed the book shut. Bruce reached across the table and grabbed it. He began flipping the pages.

"We need some help with this," she muttered.

Bruce glanced up from the book at Trudy. He looked shocked. "You okay?"

"No." She had her arms crossed over her chest and tears stained her reddened cheeks.

He closed the book. "It's okay. We'll get someone to help us."

"Who can help us? Besides, I don't know if I really want to know everything," she said between trembling lips.

"We can go back to the house and ask Alice. She might know the names of some of these initials. I already asked Sparkle…"

She stared at him at silently. His words sometimes didn't fit his appearance. No, there was much more to this bookkeeper than he was letting on. She didn't trust him, but she would have to work with him; she couldn't do this alone.

"Okay, let's go." She rose from her chair and he grabbed the bill before she could.

"I'll pay for this," he said.

"Now, Bruce, that's not fair. You're helping me, so I should pay." Not that she didn't wish she could just let him pay, due to her increasingly desperate financial situation.

"How about Dutch?"

She shrugged. "Okay."

She retrieved her brown faux leather purse from the floor beneath her seat, popped it open, and reached inside for her wallet. She flipped it open, and there opposite her credit cards was a picture of her and Rocky, standing in front of the fireplace at their home in Seattle. The picture had been taken five years ago at Christmastime.

He was in his best navy suit and she in the long evening dress he'd bought for her that year. It was still her favorite outfit.

The bare back made her feel sexy. She recalled the warmth of the fire on her skin while posing for that picture. She could still smell the smoke from the crackling wood. A sense of sadness threatened to overwhelm her.

Why had they left their home? Why had they moved here? How had she failed Rocky, shoving him into the arms of another woman?

Bruce left the table, walked to the reception area, and now stood at the cashier's desk. Smiling weakly, she left the table to join him. She pulled a ten-dollar bill from her wallet. "Is this enough?" she asked.

He nodded.

The manager rang the total through the cash register. He looked at them without emotion, stone-faced as Bruce set down two tens and waited while the manager gave him the change, which he handed to Trudy. She waved it away, but he pushed it at her. After giving him a sheepish grin, she put the change in her wallet.

Once outside, she was pleased to see the clouds had started to break; now thin streaks of golden sunlight shot through the gray overcast. Steam rose from the asphalt parking lot like ghosts rising in a graveyard.

They walked to the car and got in. Bruce managed to get in without hitting his head. Trudy grinned at him as the engine turned over on the first turn of the key. Things were getting better. She hoped.

Thirteen

Rocky was released with a warning and instructed not to leave town. Rocky had smirked. Where the hell would he go? That young cop was a real hard-ass with his empty threats. Rocky didn't care for threats, not that they had anything on him.

A light rain had begun to fall. Peering up at the pale gray clouds covering the sky horizon to horizon, he shook his head. Did it always have to rain in this damn town?

He had wanted to move farther south. Somewhere in California or Florida would have been nice, but Trudy had insisted on Oregon. Damn weather made his bones ache just like Seattle had. Would he ever feel warm again?

Pulling his keys from the pocket of his sport coat, he approached his blue pickup. He unlocked the door and climbed in. The bench seat sighed under his weight.

The interior smelled of stale beer and cigarettes. There were old, fast-food wrappers scattered on the floor of the truck where he'd thrown them. He was getting quite a collection.

Every fast food joint in the known universe was represented.

Slipping the key into the ignition, he started the truck. The V8 engine roared to life. Revving it once, he pulled the gearshift toward him until it was in reverse, then backed up while looking in the rearview mirror to make sure he didn't hit anything. The last thing he needed right now was a fender bender in the parking lot of the sheriff's station.

Once stopped and after shifting into drive, he stepped on the gas and drove out of the gravel parking lot onto the highway. He had to get home. Trudy would be expecting him. He drove slower than usual because he needed to plan what he was going to say to her. She would be really pissed, not that he blamed her. He knew he had been an ass of the first order.

He decided to blame the booze. It impaired his judgment. Yeah, that might work. And he'd promise to stop drinking—well, at least cut back. Trudy would like that.

He smiled to himself. "Always lie to your wife," that's what his friends back home told him when they'd been playing poker every Friday night. This was all her fault anyway; Trudy had talked him into selling his business and moving to Fairview.

The light at the next intersection turned red, forcing him to stop.

He glanced in the rear view mirror in time to see a plain brown Ford sedan back a couple of blocks pull into an empty parking space. He saw there was a lone occupant in the car. It must be that nosy woman cop. His old anger burned inside him. Sanchez was a fucking bitch and obviously a dyke who hated men.

When the light changed, he hit the accelerator a little too hard, and the back end of his truck fishtailed before he pulled his foot away and the truck settled on the road. The car beside him honked and the driver waved his fist at him.

Rocky shrugged sheepishly.

After leaving the highway at his turnoff, he drove to the house he and Trudy shared. Pulling into the driveway behind Trudy's Chevette, he stopped and cut the truck's engine. He scowled at her car.

It was the middle of the day and she was usually at the shop. He frowned. How were they supposed to pay the bills if she was home instead of bringing in the bacon?

Exiting the truck, he slammed the car door, then went to the house.

Just as he was about to put his brass key into the lock, the door suddenly swung open and he was face-to-face with a large man with shoulder-length black hair, a beard, and a mustache. His youthful face was twisted in anger and his dark eyes bored into him.

The guy was dressed like a biker. For a fleeting moment, Rocky thought Fairview might have been invaded by a renegade bike gang, like the town in a Marlon Brando movie from his youth.

"Are you Rocky Wilson?"

The man's baritone timber knotted his belly in fear. The guy sounded as scary as he looked.

"Uh... yeah," Rocky's voice trembled in his ears.

"We wanna talk to you." The man grabbed him by the lapels of his sport coat and pulled him inside, very nearly lifting him off his feet.

A familiar voice said his name from the landing at the top of the stairs. He couldn't see her, but he knew she was there.

"Put him down, Bruce, and bring him upstairs." It was Trudy. Relief washed over him. I'm saved, he thought.

Bruce let go of him, waving him toward the staircase leading to the upper level of the split-level house.

Rocky nodded. Starting up the stairs, he was followed closely by the massive biker. He entered the living room, where Trudy sat in the recliner near the front window. It was almost as if she'd planned for his arrival and staged it.

Anger tightened his stomach muscles.

"What the hell is going on here?" he asked.

Bruce took a step closer to him, his dark eyes glaring, staring him down. Rocky took a step back and his mouth dried.

"It's okay, Bruce," said Trudy dryly. Her eyes were flat, expressionless.

Bruce motioned toward the living room couch. It was an old tweed couch they'd brought with them from Seattle. As he sat down, he could smell tea brewing in the kitchen. He hated the stuff. Beer was his beverage of choice. Tea was for old ladies and pansies.

"Would you like some tea, Bruce?" asked Trudy, giving the large man a warm smile.

He nodded grimly, keeping his eyes focused on Rocky as if he were a meal fit for a rabid dog.

Rocky decided to change his mind about tea. "May I have some too, dear?"

Her expression changed to a glare. "You're fucking kidding, right?"

Rocky smiled weakly as he nodded. She walked away. He watched her go, the rustle of her slacks echoing as she moved across the living room until she disappeared into the kitchen.

In a few moments that seemed like hours, she returned carrying two white mugs filled with steaming tea. She handed one to Bruce, who uncrossed his muscular arms from across his massive chest, smiled thinly, and thanked her, all the while not taking his eyes off Rocky.

It was the first words the biker had said since they'd come into the living room.

Trudy crossed the room, taking a seat in the high-backed, cloth-covered recliner. She arranged her white-sock-covered feet underneath her, holding her teacup in her right hand. All the while, Trudy stared over the cup at Rocky as she blew air across the rim to cool the tea.

Her composed look made him tremble inside. She was making him sweat.

"I think we have some things to talk about," Trudy said, breaking her silence. She took small sips; finally she lowered the mug from her lips.

"Yeah, I guess so," he said, avoiding her incessant stare.

Bruce grunted.

Rocky watched her turn her head slightly and nod to the large man. He grimaced and walked out of the room into the kitchen to leave them alone to discuss the future of their marriage.

Rocky knew this was the moment of truth. He was uncertain. Trudy was a great woman, but maybe he needed more. He didn't know exactly what he wanted. Was this why all those books and Oprah shows talked about the midlife crisis?

"Why?" asked Trudy, speaking in a hoarse whisper.

It was a simple question, but he saw the unmistakable pain in her eyes. So many years together had attuned him to her feelings. They knew each other so well. Maybe that was the problem. Was he bored? Was that why he'd run around with Sharon?

His gut twisted at the thought of the buxom blonde lying naked in his arms. She was dead, not only to him but to all the others, as well. She hadn't thought he'd known, but he knew everything about her.

She'd accused him of being a stalker a few times, but he'd managed to deflect her anger by feigning surprise and hurt at her suggestion. She'd said she'd saved every note and recorded every phone call from him, suggesting if he didn't do what she wanted, Trudy would hear the tapes and see the notes. She'd played him like a fiddle, and like an over-sexed schoolboy, he'd fallen for her. Sharon had been his forbidden fruit.

The familiar anger returned at being used by her. He was just another stupid man, used by a manipulative bitch.

Trudy must have sensed his thoughts because she frowned and her face flushed. "Well, you gonna tell me or not?"

"No," he said, shaking his head. "I'm just upset about everything that's happened and all."

"Because that bitch is dead," Trudy said, her voice bitter.

Rocky lowered his hands to his sides and moved forward on the couch, then clasped his hands in front of him. "I'm so sorry, Trud. I've made a real mess of things and I let you down."

"Yes, you did," she agreed, nodding.

He winced. "I'll make it up to you somehow. I'll stop drinking and I'll never cheat on you again. I promise."

Trudy stared at him, her face impassive. "Did you kill her?"

"You think I'd do something like that? Me?"

She shook her head. "Of course not. But,if it wasn't you, then who did?"

Bruce reappeared from the kitchen where he'd been listening to their conversation. "That's what I want to know, too."

There was a knock on the front door. They all froze and stared at each other.

"I'll see who it is," offered Trudy.

Before Bruce or Rocky could move, she hurried down the stairs and was looking out the peephole. She was surprised to see Detective Sanchez standing on the front stoop.

Trudy undid the deadbolt and removed the brass chain from the slot. Bruce had locked both to keep Rocky from escaping until she got to the bottom of his involvement in Sharon's death.

After forcing a smile to her lips, she swung the door open. "Yes, Detective, what can I do for you?"

"May I come in? Kinda damp and cold out here." Sanchez's hands were buried in the pockets of her tan suit jacket. She had her best cop-on-a-case smile, one Trudy was certain had opened many a door for her.

"Actually, we're kinda busy," said Trudy, nodding toward the stairs. "My hubby just got home." She winked knowingly.

Sanchez grinned. "It'll only take a few minutes of your time." Sanchez wasn't taking no for an answer.

"Okay."

Sanchez nodded, walked in, and followed Trudy up the stairs. When they got to the living room, Bruce was nowhere in sight and Rocky stood near the couch, his hands in the pockets of his sport coat, shuffling his feet nervously side to side.

"Why, hello again, Mr. Wilson," said Sanchez, the sarcasm evident in her tone. The bulge of her automatic pistol, secured in the holster on her belt, was clearly visible on her right hip beneath her jacket.

"Would you like to sit down?" Rocky said.

Sanchez nodded, then sat in the recliner, her thin arms resting flat on the arms, crossing her long legs.

Rocky sat down and Trudy sat on the couch next to him. She didn't trust this cop.

"I think you know why I'm here," said Sanchez, her dark eyes focused on the couple who had slid away from each other to opposite ends of the couch.

"Husbands cheat on their wives every day," said Trudy, "there's no crime in that."

Sanchez nodded. "No. You're right. But murder, and conspiracy to commit murder, are crimes—ones which I specialize in investigating."

"Well, as I understand it, Sharon was on the beach last night and her death is an accident," said Trudy

Sanchez shook her head. "No. I don't think so. And I think your husband knows more than he's telling you." Sanchez's eyes narrowed. "You, Mrs. Wilson, I'm not so sure about."

Trudy glared at Rocky, then turned to face Sanchez. "Detective Sanchez," she said in a carefully measured tone. "I don't think my husband killed anyone. He's a cheater and a coward, as you can clearly see." She waved a dismissive hand at Rocky. "And if you think I had anything to do with her death, then you are mistaken. Now, unless there's anything else, I think it's time you left." Trudy stood, as did Sanchez.

Sanchez held out her hand, which Trudy ignored then turned and led the way to the stairs. Sanchez followed her.

"You're making a mistake," said Sanchez as she walked through the front door onto the cement landing at the top of the three stone steps between the walkway and the paved driveway.

"I don't think so. That's where you and I disagree." Trudy closed the door, listening intently to Sanchez's retreating footsteps as she returned to her car. Trudy stayed near the door, barely breathing until she heard the car's engine start, followed by the hum of the tires as the car backed out and drove away.

Her breathing returned to normal and she went back upstairs.

Bruce stood leaning against one wall, his eyes focused again on Rocky, whose shoulders now trembled from the sobs wracking his body. His head was bowed, his eyes closed tightly.

"Pathetic," said Bruce, shaking his head.

"Yeah, isn't he?" asked Trudy, standing with her arms crossed over her body. "Where were you?"

Trudy's eyes narrowed and her brow wrinkled. "I think she knows something we don't. Any ideas?"

Bruce shrugged. "But I agree with you. What about him?" Rocky had stopped crying and he was watching them. Trudy recognized the look in his eye.

"Oh, for heaven's sake," Trudy said. "You stupid son of a bitch. Bruce isn't my lover, he's Sharon's brother."

Rocky's eyes popped wide and a look of fear came into them. He began to tremble. "I didn't know." His voice was a whisper. "Look, I didn't have anything to do with Sharon's disappearance. I didn't even know she was missing and presumed dead until the cop told me."

Trudy's eyebrows arched and her eyes shifted to Bruce. "Presumed? That puts things in a different light."

Bruce nodded. "Yeah. This means they have some evidence that her disappearance wasn't an accident. Maybe it's the shoe we talked about earlier. And it means someone reported her missing. It wasn't me so who?"

Rocky looked at them with a curious expression. "You mean the red ones?"

Trudy nodded. She didn't want to say what Sharon called them in front of Sharon's brother, but they were "fuck me" shoes.

Disgust twisted her stomach in knots. She knew where her husband had seen Sharon's shoes, under her bed.

A frown crossed Rocky's blotchy features and his eyes narrowed. "She only wore those on special occasions."

Trudy turned away so her husband couldn't see the pain in her eyes. This was all too much.

"But what else do they have?" asked Bruce, smoothly changing the subject when he sensed Trudy's pain.

"I dun' know..." began Rocky, but he stopped abruptly and his eyes went wide again. He snapped his fingers. "I know," he said, his voice excited. "The tapes. The cops msut have found them when they searched Sharon's room." His eyes travelled between Trudya nd Bruce. "I mean they must have searched her room, right?"

"How many tapes were there?" asked Bruce.

"Well, I don't know, exactly. Sharon once told me she recorded every phone call she ever received—just in case—whatever that meant." Rocky shrugged and looked away from Trudy's and Bruce's stares.

Trudy steeled herself. "Would you be on those tapes?"

Rocky lowered his eyes and his voice. "I guess so. Do you think that's why the cops think I did something to her?"

"Depends on what you said," said Bruce as he moved to stand beside Trudy and put a meaty hand on her shoulder, then whisper something in her left ear. He stepped back when she nodded.

Her eyes brimmed with tears, forcing her blink to blink them away. "Now, I need you to think carefully, Rock. Did you ever say anything that might make someone think you wanted to hurt Sharon?"

He shrugged. "Yeah, maybe... uh... probably... I don't know, exactly. I said a lot of things when I was—"

"Drunk," interrupted Bruce. Rocky nodded.

Bruce rolled his eyes. "Trudy, maybe we should talk to Emily and Alice to see if they know what was on those tapes."

Trudy glared at Rocky. "You stay here, stud, while Bruce and I check this out. Understood?"

Rocky sighed and nodded.

"And try to stay out of trouble while I'm gone. That cop would love an excuse to bust your ass."

"How long are you gonna be gone?" Rocky asked.

"As long as it takes," said Bruce, glaring at Rocky. Rocky shrank before the big man's gaze.

Trudy walked toward the hallway. "Before we go, I'm gonna have a quick shower and change into some fresh clothes. I've gotta get the perm solution smell off me," she said before disappearing down the hallway.

***

Bruce sat in the recliner, studying Rocky. He was a little tired after a late night. He recalled Emily's smooth, silky skin in his hands and the gentle moans that escaped from her full lips as they made love. He forced her from his mind by concentrating on Rocky.

Now was not the time for him to be thinking about his latest conquest. His beloved sister had been murdered, and despite what Trudy thought, as far as he was concerned, this scumbag remained a suspect.

But doubts remained. This overweight, balding, middle-aged man didn't look like the type who ran around on his wife, never mind killing anyone, though looks could be deceiving. Sharon must have thought Rocky had something, but he couldn't see it.

He sighed to himself. There was no accounting for his sister's taste in men.

"So, why?" he asked.

Rocky shrugged. "Why what?"

"I think you know."

"Your sister was fun, exciting. I liked her." The echo of running water from the bathroom stopped.

"I loved my sister," said Bruce after long silence, "faults and all. She was a slut, but that doesn't matter to me. I loved her. Unconditionally."

"Well, if it's any consolation, I loved her, too."

Bruce shifted forward in his chair.

Trudy walked into the room, dressed, ready to head out. She smelled like lavender and had donned a pair of faded blue jeans and a gray University of Washington Husky's sweatshirt. As well, she carried a small, sky-blue travel bag with while nylon straps.

"How're you boys getting along?" she asked.

"Fine. Aren't we?" asked Bruce, eyeing Rocky.

"Yeah, sure. We're fine. Where're you going?" he asked, nodding at the travel bag.

"We may have to go to Newport for a couple of days," she said.

Bruce nodded grimly.

"What about the shop?"

Spinning to face her husband, she glared at him but didn't reply. Instead, she turned away and walked to the closet near the top of the stairs.

The wooden accordion door slats gleamed in the dim light of the living room. The track was worn, so it needed a firm pull to open. Trudy slid the door open and took her faux leather coat off the wire hangar.

Slipping it on over the sweatshirt, she zipped the coat closed.

"Since when did you give a shit about the shop?" Not waiting for an answer, she started down the stairs.

Before Bruce followed her, he stopped and pointed a single index finger at Rocky and then at his own chest. He mouthed the word, "later," then hurried down the stairs in time to open the front door for Trudy.

***

The door slammed behind them and Rocky was alone. He dropped back onto the couch and heaved a heavy sigh. His wife and the biker brother of his dead lover were digging into the past, and he didn't like it one bit. Trudy would find out all about him and Sharon. He needed a drink.

Fourteen

EMILY CROSS, THE SMALL-TOWN GIRL FROM IOWA, held the cigarette to her red lips, drawing in a deep drag. Her head was slightly cocked to one side. She sat on the couch facing the front window. The acrid smoke curled from between her lips as she released it from her lungs. Her eyes were closed.

One bare leg was folded underneath her cutoffs, and the purple tube top she wore strained to hold her full breasts. She was proud of her girls and considered them her best asset. Men usually agreed with her.

Bruce seemed like a nice guy. She liked him, but then again, like Sharon, she liked most men. She wondered why Sharon had taken up with that loser Rocky Wilson, though. He was a slob, a drunk, and not too bright.

Maybe she'd wanted to get control of that hair shop. Sharon had often said she wanted to own her own shop one day. Emily smirked. Sharon had said a lot of things.

Maybe I should give Bruce the tapes Sharon made of her phone calls? He might be able to use them, they are his now anyway.

She wasn't about to give them to those creepy cops.

Those damn cops had been very nosy about her roomie when they'd ransacked the house. They'd said she was missing and maybe dead or something. Emily had almost laughed aloud at that. Sharon was always off on one of her adventures. Many a time she'd disappeared for days, shacking up with some guy and then coming home looking like she'd been ridden hard then thrown out with the trash.

Emily's ears perked up when she heard the squeak of brakes being applied and the sound of a throaty engine dying off in the driveway. Opening her eyes, she stood up and walked to the door.

The coal-black sky and cool wind made her shiver. It was late afternoon and it would be night soon. She couldn't make out who was in the blue truck parked outside. She had seen the truck before and knew it wasn't Rocky's. That scumbag had hit on her more than once, but he was too old and creepy for her tastes.

She padded back to the couch on her bare feet and sat down again to wait for the doorbell. There was a knock, accompanied by the sound of breaking glass. The exterior light on the landing went out.

She stood, shrugged, and then walked to the door, still holding the lit cigarette, its trail of white smoke following her. Flinging open the door, she intended to raise some serious shit over the light bulb. Those damn things were expensive.

Her anger turned to fear when a figure dressed in a black leather jacket, black gloves, and a black balaclava appeared in front of her.

A scream caught in her throat when she spotted the long-bladed knife in the right hand of the strange figure. The knife flashed toward her. Instantly, blinding pain shot across her neck. Dropping the cigarette, her hands went to her throat.

Something warm and sticky flowed over her fingers. Her knees became weak and she struggled to remain upright, leaning against the door frame.

Her vision clouded and she shivered. It's so cold....

Her final thought before the darkness enveloped her was, why?

***

Emily was dead before her shapely body collapsed into a heap in the open doorway. Her neck and chest were coated with her own blood.

The dark figure wiped the bloody blade on her tube top, then walked away, returning to the truck, getting in, and starting the engine.

The blue pickup truck disappeared behind a stand of pine trees lining the road. In its wake, the hopes and dreams of Emily Cross lay in a pool of her own cooling blood.

***

Trudy stopped the Chevette in the driveway in front of the blue-and-white cottage. It was dark now. She frowned when she saw that the front door was open and a lump of something lay framed by the light coming from inside. The lump, whatever it was, looked odd.

Bruce stepped out of the car and cocked his head. "The cover on the porch light near the door is broken," he said. "What's that in the doorway?"

Together, he and Trudy started walking toward the house until they froze when they recognized the shape in the entrance. The lump was human.

Trudy's heart began to race as she recognized the dark hair and the clothes. It must be Emily.

Bruce raced to squat beside her and held up her left wrist to check for a pulse. He looked at Trudy when she joined him and shook his head. Emily's unseeing eyes were wide open and the look in them made her shudder. She had seen whoever killed her, too late.

The front of her purple tube top was covered in blood so Bruce's hands and the cuffs of his blue jeans were stained with her blood, too. There wasn't as much as Trudy would have expected. Emily's throat had been cut and she had bled out.

Trudy's hands trembled and her face felt cold. "Do you think whoever did this is still around? Maybe we should call the cops?"

Bruce rose from his haunches to stand over the body of his sister's friend. He nodded. "Yeah, but I'm gonna kill the son of a bitch before the cops get here," he said between gritted teeth. His face was flushed and his large shoulders trembled. He turned toward Trudy.

She gazed at him through watery eyes. "What the hell is going on?"

He shook his head while his eyes scanned the empty street. A few of the houses near them had outside lights on.

The air was rife with the odor of blood, making Trudy queasy. She swallowed the bile at the back of her throat, trying to keep her last meal down. She'd never seen such brutality first hand.

Unable to hold back any longer, she stumbled down the painted cement steps toward a green hedge, then dropped to her knees and emptied the contents of her stomach.

Bruce came up behind her and held her shoulders as her body heaved. When her stomach was empty, the heaving stopped. She began to cry, her body wracked by long sobs.

"She was so young," she gasped.

Bruce patted her shoulders with his big hands. "Trudy, it's okay."

"No, it's not. Maybe she's dead because of us." Trudy said in a burst of anger.

"That's bull and you know it," he said.

"Is it?" She shook her head. "Oh, Rocky…"

"You think he did this?" Bruce said bitterly. "He's not strong enough to have done this. Sorry, but your lazy ass husband is a two hundred pound pile of pudding."

She looked into his dark eyes. "What do you mean?" Her hazel eyes narrowed.

He shrugged. "It takes a strong person to kill someone with a knife. Especially with one stroke across the neck. Whoever did this almost slashed through her neck to her spine. That takes strength."

She sat back on her haunches and he released her shoulders. "I'm not following. What are you, a fucking cop now all of a sudden?"

He smiled thinly. "Naw, it's just that I've seen a few knife fights in my day, back home, and this one's a pro job if I've ever seen one."

"Why would a professional killer want Emily dead? She's a nobody."

"I didn't mean to suggest the killer is a professional, I'm saying whoever did this knows how to use a knife."

Trudy nodded. Her husband hadn't killed Emily. That didn't mean he hadn't killed Sharon, but that, too, was beginning to look doubtful now that this had happened. Someone was really pissed. They could be next.

Suddenly a police siren echoed in the distance. The cops were on their way. Not that it mattered at the moment but who made the call? Trudy was beginning to think someone was pulling the strings around here to deflect attention from themselves.

Bruce winced. "This is gonna get messy."

Trudy nodded. "Yeah."

Trudy knew Sanchez wasn't going to like them being at the murder scene, with big Bruce here having Emily's blood on him. As they had no motive, it was unlikely any charges would stick, but it wasn't going to be easy or pretty.

The more difficult question, now that Emily—one of the few people who might know what the initials in Sharon's black book meant—was dead, was how would they solve the murder before Sanchez had her and Rocky behind bars?

And the answering machine tapes held untold secrets that only Sanchez would know. Trudy glanced at Bruce, who had his hands buried in his pockets, waiting for the cops to arrive.

It dawned on her that there was one other living person who might know something. Who might be able to help. And they had to get to her before Sanchez, or the killer, did. Someone was closing loose ends. They had to stop whoever it was before it was too late.

Fifteen

DOLORES SANCHEZ STARED AT THE BLOODY CORPSE lying in the bungalow's doorway. She sank to her haunches to closely examine the woman's body. The air still had that talcum powder smell from the gloves she'd put on moments before.

The coroner had requested they take pictures, and Summers had already snapped off a roll, from various angles, of the dark-haired woman lying in the pool of blood.

As she lifted away the victim's red-stained arm, she saw the deep cut across the neck that had robbed this pretty young woman of her life. The insertion point was in line with the right ear and ran across the throat, ending under the left ear. The killer had cut deep enough that the head was nearly severed. The woman had clearly drowned in her own blood. While it was obvious what had happened here, the coroner's autopsy would determine exactly when and where the fatal blow had been struck. It was procedure.

The woman had bled out very quickly. And the manner of the cutting of the throat meant the woman wouldn't have been able to scream with the blood choking her.

The dead woman's eyes were fixed and sightless, gazing into eternity.

According to Trudy Wilson and the guy she was with, who'd identified himself—and his green-and-white Washington State Driver's license had confirmed—as Bruce Carstairs, brother to Sharon, the other missing and possibly murdered woman. They said this woman's name was Emily, one of Sharon's roommates. They didn't know her last name.

Small towns weren't what they used to be. Sanchez gently shut Emily's eyes with her gloved fingers.

She stood up. "We gotta move her to the morgue," she said to Summers.

Summers nodded. "Yeah, 'cept we gotta take her to Eugene. We got no morgue here."

This would mean another delay. This investigation was going to take longer than ever now. Just when she'd thought she had the case wrapped up, someone had thrown her another curve. A second murder of the three roommates was more than a coincidence.

"Okay, get the ambulance guys to take the body to Eugene. And call the coroner; tell him I need a rush on the results. We have two possible murders and only one body, which might have the evidence we need to solve them both."

Summers nodded to the two ambulance attendants standing at the bottom of the cement stairs. One had a vinyl body bag thrown over his left arm. Between them was a wheeled stretcher.

Sanchez and Summers moved down the steps to watch the attendants lift the corpse into the body bag, then pull the zipper closed. They lifted it onto the stretcher, then rolled it to the driveway and the waiting ambulance, parked behind Sanchez's car.

Sanchez and Summers removed their protective gloves. Sanchez's eyes studied the now empty doorway.

"Who owns this place?" she asked.

Summers flipped open his notebook to the place where he'd recorded Bruce's and Trudy's statements earlier.

They'd let them go because it was obvious they hadn't been involved in this murder. Bruce had some blood on him, but not enough; given the victim's blood loss, the murderer should be covered in blood. And while Bruce had plenty of strength, he'd barely known the girl, though he had slept with her recently. As far as Sanchez could determine, he didn't have a motive for her murder. It didn't add up in her mind.

Sanchez and Summers had searched the area around the house and not found any weapons or a blood trail.

"Carstairs and Wilson said they didn't know who owned the place, but the third roommate work's at Al's. I put a call in to the station, asking them to call her and tell her to come home right away."

"Al's? What's that?" asked Sanchez.

Summers glanced up from his notebook, a wry smile on his lips. "Sorry, Al's Spaghetti Barn. It's a tourist trap on the coast highway. Carstairs said the girl's a waitress."

Sanchez nodded. They would just have to wait. In the meantime, they'd have to do some good, old-fashioned investigative grunt work and interview the neighbors. One of them had called the cops, and hopefully someone might have seen something.

"Come on, we're gonna knock on some doors." She pointed to the right side of the street. "You take the right, I'll take the left."

Summers gazed at the row of bungalows that disappeared from sight over a rise, running down the right side of the rain-slicked street. Some had lights on inside while others were dark. "All of them?"

Sanchez looked at him with a sour expression on her face. "You're a cop, aren't you?" He didn't respond. She waved her left hand at the row of houses. "So this is real police work."

Without another word, she started toward the first house on the left side of the street. Summers grumbled to himself as he headed for the nearest house on the right.

They left the door to the blue-and-white bungalow open. The yellow police tape and red stains in the doorway were the only remaining evidence of the life that had once been there.

***

Bruce drove the Chevette, hunched over the wheel. It was the only way he could sit, given the seat wouldn't go back any farther. He squinted through the smeary windshield; the worn wipers were doing a poor job clearing the hard rain that struck the windshield.

Bruce was weary from the two-hour interrogation by Detective Sanchez, and driving this sorry excuse for a car made him edgy. At least the detective allowed him to wash the blood off his hands, but dark stains remained on the cuffs of his jeans.

The detective had been satisfied that they hadn't murdered poor Emily, but she eyed them suspiciously when they said they were riding together. No doubt Sanchez thought they'd become lovers, something neither Trudy nor Bruce made any attempt to correct.

Let her think what she wanted to.

It would keep her wondering and hopefully off balance until he and Trudy discovered who killed his sister and they cleared Trudy as a suspect.

When they arrived at the junction where the road met the highway, Bruce brought the car to a shuddering stop. He cringed. At least it stopped. The traffic was heavy; he would have to wait. Does the constant traffic ever ease up? he wondered.

"So, which way?" he asked, his eyes intent on the cars and motor homes splashing water over them as they rushed passed. Finally, an opening came and Bruce stepped hard on the gas pedal. The Chevette shuddered and sputtered, then the engine caught, shooting them forward into the flow without becoming a hood ornament for the forty-foot motor home bearing down on them.

"Head north," Trudy murmured before closing her eyes, her arms hugging her body.

"Fuck," said Bruce.

Trudy nodded. "Going south, big fella?"

Bruce grunted in reply. He turned into a side road so he could turn them around. In a few minutes they were headed north.

"Stop here." Trudy grunted when he again stopped and turned off the engine. The only noises now were the buzz of wet tires on pavement as cars rushed past them and the rain striking the roof of the car.

"So we goin' to Newport or not?" he asked. Bruce was getting more and more short with Trudy as his anger about this situation grew. First his sister and now his newest lover were dead, murdered by someone unknown.

"Bruce," Trudy said gently, "I realize this may not be the best time, but if we're going to find the killer, we need to do something first. Then we'll go to Newport. Okay?"

He nodded, but wasn't happy. They might be putting Alice's life in danger. They weren't cops.

Trudy opened her eyes and nodded toward the restaurant on her side of the car. Bruce followed her gaze and nodded. The brown- and green-shingled single-story building with the Christmas lights strung around the low roof overhang was reported to serve the best Italian food on the coast. At least, that's what the sign on the highway claimed.

Bruce got out and followed her until they were under the overhang out of the rain. They walked side by side (the walkway extended far enough to cover both of them) until they reached the twin oak front doors for Al's Spaghetti Barn.

Bruce pulled one door open and held it for Trudy until she entered the dimly lit interior. He went in after, then let the door swing closed behind him. As their eyes adjusted to the dim lighting conditions, they saw the square tables. Each had a wine bottle with a candle stuck in it.

He'd never been in this restaurant, but it looked a little touristy and clearly wasn't authentic Italian. Cheaply framed paintings of Italian scenery hung from dark wood paneling; a tinny speaker system warbled opera music. The place smelled of tinned tomato sauce and over-cooked macaroni and cheese.

An older, heavyset woman with tightly rolled gray hair stacked on top of her head, wearing a blue flowered dress covered by a clean white apron, approached them. Her brown eyes sparkled when she greeted them.

"Two, for dinner?" she asked. Her accent was more Brooklyn than Italy, but she probably knew good Italian food if she came from New York.

Trudy smiled warmly. "Actually, no. We're looking for Alice."

121

The woman's expression changed to one of concern. She clasped her large hands together across her expansive apron. "Alice, poor thing." The woman eyes lowered to look at the floor. "She left when the call came."

"What call?" asked Bruce, a little too forcefully because the woman appeared startled.

"Uh... from the police, of course," she said, her voice trembling. "I hope they found her roommate," she added, obviously referring to Sharon, because no one outside them and the cops knew about poor Emily.

"Shit," Bruce muttered . He grabbed Trudy by the arm and rushed her toward the double oak doors.

"Thank you," said Trudy, sounding cheerful.

Soon they were in the car headed back to the rented house, hoping to get there in time to protect Alice. Two women were dead, she might be next. Bruce crouched over the steering wheel, concentrating on the dark pavement and driving as fast as he could through the traffic. A knot of fear the size of a baseball had formed in his stomach.

They had to find Alice—fast—before she was the next victim on The Price Is Too High. A once quiet Oregon coast town that had been a retreat for many had become a place of danger and death where no one was safe.

Sixteen

Bruce and Trudy arrived just as Alice was getting out of her car outside the bungalow. They saw her brow furrow in the headlights' beams when they pulled up behind her yellow, two-door Toyota.

Bruce turned off the engine, opened the door, and shot out of the car. Folding the driver's seat forward, he waved to Alice. "Get in," he said, his tone urgent.

Alice stared uncomprehending at him, then turned toward the open door of the bungalow. Her eyes went wide when she saw the shiny, banana-yellow police tape across the door and a dark stain running down the gray cement steps. "What happened?" she asked. The metallic stench of blood still hung thick in the air.

"Do what he says," said Trudy, hurrying toward the stunned woman. After reaching her side, Trudy grasped Alice's narrow shoulders with both hands. Trudy thought for a moment Alice might be in shock because she didn't say anything. She also didn't move.

"Alice." Trudy whispered. "I know this is a great shock." A look of puzzlement crossed the younger woman's face.

"What are you talking about?" asked the blonde. Her look changed to one of horror. "Have they found Sharon?"

Trudy shook her head. "No, not yet. But they did find Emily." She nodded toward the open door. "Up there."

Alice looked into Trudy's eyes. "Of course, silly, that's where she lives." She shook free of Trudy's grasp, then started for the house.

Bruce rushed to grab her left arm and stop her before she could reach the stairs. "Sparkle's dead—murdered," he said in a monotone voice.

Alice froze, looking into his now pleading eyes. Her expression softened as she realized he wasn't lying to her. He'd used Emily's nickname, which meant he and Emily had been friends of a sort.

Tears began to well in her eyes and she began to tremble. "Oh, my God…"

"And you're next unless we get you the fuck outta here," said Bruce. He looked for and found that the two cop cars were still here. They were probably interviewing the neighbors, so they still had time to get Alice out of here before the cops returned.

"Come on," urged Trudy, rushing toward her car. Bruce wrapped one massive arm around Alice, who sagged into his shoulder, sobbing uncontrollably.

Trudy got behind the wheel while Bruce helped Alice in behind the passenger seat. After he'd pushed the seat back into position, he ducked his head to get in himself. This time he didn't quite make it and again banged his head on the doorframe.

"Owww. Son of a bitch." He pulled the door of the Chevette closed just as Trudy started the engine. She quickly backed the car up, turned, and headed away from the house.

"What about my car?" asked Alice through her tears.

"It's better if we travel together," said Trudy, glancing at Bruce, who nodded grimly, his right hand rubbing the spot where the metal frame had clipped his scalp.

"Oh," said Alice, evidently accepting Trudy's explanation since she was still in shock. Once they were headed south on the highway toward Newport, Trudy planned to pull over to the side of the highway. She kept a blanket in the trunk for emergencies; she would give it to Alice. She had learned at a first aid course she had taken that victims of shock need to be kept warm.

By the time they were on the highway and Trudy had found a place to pull off, Alice had fallen asleep. Surprisingly, she snored—loudly.

Trudy grinned at Bruce, who shrugged. Trudy offered Bruce the keys to open the hatch. He climbed out of the cramped car and stretched himself to his full height. Trudy had a rush of sympathy for the man. It was going to be a long trip with him crammed inside the little car.

Now she wished she had Rocky's pickup. While it only had room for three people, at least it had sufficient headroom for men Bruce's size.

Bruce moved around the back of the car and slipped the key into the lock. She heard him rummaging around in the back until he poked his head over the seat. His eyes reflected a little frustration. "It's not here. I thought you said…"

Trudy opened her door. She stepped on the wet pavement and walked around the car to join him, standing in front of the open hatch. She shoved aside the piles of old clothes she kept there and the box containing a flashlight, a green metal box with even darker green block letters on it that said "First Aid," an extra bottle of blue washer fluid, and a blue plastic rain sheet. Bruce was right.

There was no blanket.

Trudy frowned. "You're right." She grunted in disgust, then pushed the hatch down until it clicked once again, locked in place.

"I don't understand; everything else is there. Why would someone take the blanket? Maybe Rocky took it for some reason," she mused.

As she spoke, Bruce walked to the driver's door. "Do you mind if I drive?"

Trudy shook her head. There was more legroom on the driver's side, and from watching his driving, he was pretty good behind the wheel.

He grinned and got in. His head was spared this time. Trudy slid in on the passenger side and closed the door.

"Onward to the promised land," she intoned in a lame attempt to inject a baritone inflection into her normally high-pitched voice.

"As you wish, mistress," said Bruce. "The game's afoot. We haven't a moment to lose." With one hand covering her mouth, Trudy managed to stifle a giggle so as not to wake the still sleeping Alice.

Bruce grinned and started the engine. He steered into traffic and they headed south once again.

Another hour, and she expected to find the answers to the incomplete puzzle of these murders. Trudy had the uncomfortable feeling that someone was pulling her strings; only this time, it wasn't Sharon who was playing her. Trudy thought she knew just where to begin her search for answers.

"I know this place in Newport where we can get a drink and a bite. You game?" he asked.

Trudy nodded. *What was the worst that could happen?*

Seventeen

IT WAS AFTER TEN O'CLOCK IN THE EVENING when the trio walked through the front door into the smoky interior of the Lap Dog Bar and Emporium in Newport. The building dated back to the fifties when (according to a plaque on the wall near the front door) it had been a beatnik coffee house. There were pot lights between the wooden beams across the ceiling.

Dark-stained, round, wooden tables were scattered haphazardly across the room. Over the tables hung low-slung metal lamps with low-watt bulbs in them, adding to the already noir ambiance. Opposite the booths, along the other wall, was an oak bar with a mirror behind it that ran the length of the wall.

A silver-haired female bartender stood behind the bar with a cigarette dangling from her dry lips. From her gray pallor and yellowed fingers, it was obvious she'd inhaled far too many cancer sticks.

At the far end of the room was a small, circular stage. On a stool on the stage, with an acoustic guitar across his lap, was a thin man dressed in head-to-toe black, with pale skin and brown, curly hair.

He was singing a low, slow, blues tune into a silver microphone on a stand in front of him.

Bruce smiled when he saw the guy on the stage. "What do you know," he said.

"You know him?" asked Trudy.

She'd wanted to go right to the hair shop where Sharon had worked before moving to Fairview. She was anxious to show the black book around to see if anyone there knew what the initials stood for. Poor Emily might have known more, but Alice, who'd woken up when they'd driven into Newport, said she didn't even know Sharon's black book existed.

She told them Emily and Sharon had been secretive about their love lives. Trudy thought the girl wasn't being completely truthful but decided Alice was still in shock, so she left the topic for now. Two roommates were dead, very likely murdered, and Alice might be next. I'd be scared outta my wits if I were her, Trudy thought.

"Yeah, I know him," Bruce responded without elaborating.

They walked to the table nearest the stage and sat down in the matching, dark-stained wooden chairs. The singer had his eyes closed as he moved through his mournful song.

After hearing only a single verse, Trudy concluded the song was about an unrequited love 'who'd done him wrong'. Why had she agreed to come here? Because we're partners and partners give and partners take. Today was her turn to give. But why this dump?

The bartender approached them. "What'll it be?" she asked, her face impassive.

They're not much on customer service, thought Trudy, eyeing the older woman's messy hair. Her haircut is a crime, and a real rat's nest.

"I'll have a light beer," said Alice, her voice bright as her smile.

Trudy eyed her. What gives with her? She shrugged. I guess shock does funny things to people. But she was no expert.

"Beer," said Bruce, his eyes fixed on the singer. "Anything you have on tap is okay." The waitress nodded.

"White wine, please," said Trudy. A thin smile played across her pursed lips. She hoped the glass was clean. The bar reeked of sweat and stale cigarette smoke.

She glanced back at Bruce, who was looking at her with a grin splitting his ruddy face.

"What's the matter? Don' you like bars? I love 'em." He turned his attention back to the stage just as the singer was finishing his song.

Bruce stood up and began to clap wildly. What the hell had gotten into him? The singer broke into a grin; his stringy curls swayed as he stepped off the stage and crossed the floor, coming toward them.

"At least someone in here loves good music," the musician said, shielding his eyes from the glare of the pot lights. As he neared the table, his features broke into a wide smile.

"B? Is it you?" The singer almost dropped his guitar as he unhooked the strap around his neck, then rushed at Bruce, who had remaining standing. Leaning the guitar against the table edge, he wrapped his arms around Bruce in a hug. Not an easy feat with a man Bruce's size.

"I gather you two know each other?" asked Trudy.

Bruce stepped back and placed a hand on the thin man's shoulder. The two looked like kids who'd just been in the candy store and made off with their loot.

"I'd like you guys to meet Tommy Roper, my oldest friend from Seattle. This son of a bitch and I went to grade school together."

"Yeah," said Tommy shaking his mop of brown curls. "This fuckin' guy and I go way back."

"Hey!" said the bartender, an angry glare on her face. "You got a show to finish, big shot."

Tommy waved to her. "All right, Ma, but I'm on a break right now."

Removing his hand from Bruce's shoulder, his eyes shifted from Trudy to Alice. "She can wait. I'd like to be introduced to your friends, ol' buddy." Before sitting in the empty chair, he yelled to the bartender to bring him a beer. "You know my brand," he added.

The old woman grumbled and turned her back to them get their drinks.

Tommy smiled thinly as he turned his attention to scanning the two women. "So, Bruce, who the frig are these two?" he asked with a twinkle in his cobalt blue eyes.

Bruce laughed. "They're okay, Tommy. We're working on something together, that's all."

"I heard about Sharon going missing on the radio," said Tommy. His expression became serious and his forehead furrowed. "Too bad. Damn shame."

"Yeah," said Bruce, casting his eyes away.

There was a moment of awkward silence before Alice decided to speak. "So you're a musician? Cool," she said her face lighting up like a kid on Christmas morning.

Tommy cocked his head toward the young blonde. "Where the hell did you pick up this bright light?"

"Hey," said Alice indignantly.

"Did we make it past the third grade?" asked Tommy sarcastically.

Trudy decided she didn't like this son of a bitch. He was a rude bastard. "We're outta here," Trudy said, standing up. "I don't have ta listen to this bullshit."

Bruce smiled thinly and motioned for Trudy to sit down. "It's okay. He's just kiddin'. Aren't you?" He glared at Tommy, who shrugged.

"Yeah. I guess so."

Trudy sat down as the sour-faced bartender appeared at the table carrying a tray of drinks. She placed their orders in front of them. Bruce was the first to take a sip from his glass.

Trudy eyed her glass of white wine. Chardonnay, or Riesling, maybe? At least the glass seemed clean enough. Whatever wine it was, it looked okay. Raising the glass to her lips, she took a tentative sip. Surprisingly, it tasted pretty good for a house wine. Who would've believed you'd find a decent wine in a place called the Lap Dog?

"How long you been workin' here, Tommy?" asked Bruce.

"Too fuckin' long. Fuckin' place is purgatory," said Tommy, his tone bitter. Bruce glared at his friend. Tommy shrugged.

"Sorry—ladies," he said. "Been in this town too long, that's all."

"How long is that?" asked Trudy.

"Five friggin' years." Tommy shook his head, then wrapped his long, narrow fingers around the brown long-necked beer bottle. Raising it to his lips, he took a long swallow.

"Did you know Sharon when she was in town?" asked Trudy.

"Of course. She's my friggin' best friend's sister." He eyed Bruce tentatively. "Besides she—" he paused. "She used to come in here all the time. She said it was like a second home."

"Did she pick up men in here?" Trudy's eyes narrowed. Maybe this guy would be useful after all. He was pretty much the crudest man she'd ever met, but he might know something important.

"Yeah. Sometimes." He glanced at Bruce, then back at Trudy. "Listen, bitch, this shit is none of your business. The chick's dead. Why don' you leave it alone?"

Bruce leaned forward and his voice lowered. "Tommy, if you know something, you better tell us."

Tommy's watery blue eyes focused on Bruce's. "Listen, ol' buddy, I don't know if you know, but Sharon—well she liked to use men who could get her—things."

"What things?" asked Trudy.

Tommy winced. "You know—things. Money, gifts, stuff like that."

"Would we know any of these men?" asked Bruce.

Tommy avoided looking at his friend. "Sharon wasn't too particular. She used to laugh about how stupid these guys were. Some were locals. Everything from lawyers to city politicos to ditch diggers. She didn't care as long as she could get laid and get something out of them in return."

Trudy's heart ached. Rocky had been a stupid fool. Sharon had used him like she'd used so many others. The only thing they had that the bitch would have wanted was the business. She recalled Sharon saying to her many times that she'd always dreamed of owning her own shop, but at her age it was probably too late.

"Why did she leave Newport?" asked Trudy.

Bruce shifted in his seat and cleared his throat. Tommy avoided Bruce's eyes, flitting instead toward the mirror behind the bar. Trudy felt the tension in the room grow. "What? Bruce," she said looking to Bruce.

She needed to know if this information might be relevant to the reason Sharon was killed, but for some reason Bruce had withheld whatever it was from her. For the first time, she thought she might've been mistaken about him.

"It's complicated," said Bruce, finally meeting her puzzled eyes.

"Well, why don't you enlighten me," she said, a frown marring her forehead. Anger rose from deep in her gut.

He shrugged. "It's like this," he began, "Sharon kinda pissed off someone who could make a lotta trouble for her. She had to get outta town before he had her tossed out."

"He who?"

"The mayor's husband," said Bruce.

Trudy knew of Newport's mayor. The first woman elected mayor of Newport made quite a splash in newspapers all up and down the coast, and beyond. "She fucked the mayor's husband?"

Alice suddenly scoffed. "You gotta be kidding. That's why she left town? What the hell could some two-bit, small-town mayor do to her?"

Trudy smiled to herself. Obviously Alice had no idea who the mayor was.

Bruce shrugged, then raised his half glass of beer and drained it before he answered. "Before she became mayor, she was head of the Oregon State Hairdressing Association. She threatened to have Sharon's state license pulled if she didn't leave town."

"She can't do that," said Trudy.

Bruce's face became grim. "Yes, she can, and almost did. Sharon thought the same as you, at least she said so when I came to visit her and offered my help. But it was too late by then, so all I did was help her pack and move to Fairview."

Tommy nodded.

Now Trudy was angry. "That makes no sense. Who does this bitch think she is that she can have so much power? I hate it when politicians throw their weight around."

Alice said, "Actually, Sharon told me there was more to her leaving than just that."

The three looked at her as if she'd suddenly grown two heads. "What are you talking about?" asked Bruce, his eyes narrowing.

"She said she had a boyfriend in Fairview who could help her with her problems with the mayor down here." Alice's eyes drifted to her still-full bottle of light beer. With trembling fingers, she picked it up, raised it to her lips, and took a quick sip, then placed the bottle back on the cardboard coaster. Trudy watched, knowing Alice was scared. Really scared.

The tension in the room returned. "Who is he?" Bruce whispered between clenched teeth, obviously struggling to keep his emotions in check.

Trudy knew that this person, whoever he was, had to be the guy they were looking for. One thing for sure, it certainly wasn't Rocky. He couldn't influence a flea in a flea circus.

Alice shrugged. "I don't know, she never told me his name. She always met him somewhere other than the house." Frowning, her eyes narrowed. "I think Emily knew."

Bruce rolled his eyes and eased back against the wooden spokes of the chair. "Well, this is great." Sighing deeply, he stood up from the table. Tommy, Alice, and Trudy also stood up.

Bruce put his free hand on his friend's shoulder. "Good to see you, Tommy." The two men hugged each other briefly, then separated. "Call me when you get up my way."

"Will do, bud." Tommy's face split into a wide grin.

Before they went out the exit, Alice turned to Tommy, her eyes quizzical. "What's an emporium?" she asked.

Tommy locked eyes with Bruce. "Big B'll tell you, I'm sure."

Outside the bar, they stood in the cool night air in the Lap Dog's parking lot, next to Trudy's car. "So who's gonna drive?" asked Bruce.

"It seems you know the territory better than we do," said Trudy, tossing him the car keys. Bruce snatched them in mid-air with his large hand.

"I know a place we can stay. And it's not no roach motel," said Bruce.

Soon they were on their way to the Beachside Motel, where Bruce had stayed when he'd visited his sister in Newport. Since it was after business hours, he'd take them to the hair shop where Sharon once worked the next day. The staff there might know something that would help them.

Trudy thought about what they'd learned from Tommy. Whoever this mystery guy was, he seemed to be the most likely suspect. Maybe they'd find out more at the hair shop tomorrow. At least she hoped so. Another dead end might mean the end of the trail and the end of her life as she knew it.

Eighteen

SITUATED ON A HILLTOP, THE BEACHSIDE MOTEL, as the name implied, overlooked a vast stretch of beach. Gray sand stretched before them like some vast desert, both to the north and the south.

Green walls of foam-capped ocean waves beat mercilessly against the gray beach as if pounding it into submission.

The motel was a two-story wooden structure painted navy blue with light gray trim.

Bruce parked the Chevette in a spot by the motel office. In front of them was a sign made from a piece of weathered driftwood, hanging over a yellow door, confirming this indeed as the office.

Since it was late, the door was closed and there was no light from inside.

It wasn't tourist season, so there would be few guests staying here.

Opening the hatch, Trudy pulled out her black leatherette shoulder bag and the bag Bruce used to carry Sharon's little black book. Before they got to Newport, they'd stopped at drugstore where Alice and Bruce bought toothbrushes. Both were in Bruce's bag.

Bruce stretched his long legs. "Damn, that piece of shit is hard on me," he said, wincing as he twisted his upper torso to remove the road kinks. Trudy blushed, a weak smile on her lips. He shrugged, looked at her, and grinned.

"I kinda like it," said Alice, a grin on her face. "It's cute."

Trudy gave Bruce an exasperated look. If this girl weren't under threat of being murdered, she didn't know if she would want her with them.

Trudy approached the office door. Recessed in the wall next to the door was a little black-and-white plastic sign, instructing after hours customers to use the button underneath to summon the manager.

Bruce walked up beside her and pushed the button. In the distance, Trudy heard the echo of a buzzer. After they waited for a few minutes and no one came, Bruce pushed the button again. The buzzer warbled once more.

"Okay, okay," said a gruff voice from somewhere overhead. "I'm comin'."

They looked up in time to see a door slam and a slim man in dark green work pants and a mustard-colored shirt start down the wooden stairs attached to the side of the building. The boards of the stairs creaked under his weight. "Can't a body have a quiet dump without some damn fool bothering him?" complained the man to no one in particular.

When he arrived at the bottom of the stairs, they saw the deep lines etched in his weathered face. A thin line of silver hair that matched his eyebrows surrounded his bald dome. "What can I do for you folks?" he asked.

"We'd like a room, please," said Bruce, a slight smile on his wide face.

"Yeah," said the man, turning toward the office door. He pulled a brass-colored key from his pants pocket and slipped it in the lock. The lock clicked as the door opened, then he led them inside.

In the office, Trudy realized immediately how warm it was. She hadn't realized how cold it was outside. The office was not only warm, but it had the homey smell of baking bread, like her grandmother's kitchen when she was a child. It may not be the most beautiful motel in the world, but it seemed Bruce knew a decent place when he saw one. She was impressed; Bruce was full of surprises.

The little reception area had two dark-stained chairs with green padded cushions, a small end table between them piled with brochures for local attractions. The man moved toward the counter, pushed aside a swinging door. The floor was covered with a burnt-orange carpet and the walls were covered with cheap pine paneling. The walls were adorned with paintings of coastal scenes with waves hitting the beach and gray-and-white seagulls floating on the breeze. The pictures weren't great art, but they were accurate.

The man opened a large black leather-bound guest book and turned it toward them. "Fill in the information, here," he pointed to the next empty space.

Bruce picked up a pen and filled in his name and address. After he was done, the man turned toward a waffle board filled with numbered keys hanging off steel hooks. Trudy noted there were two keys missing from the row where he retrieved the key for them.

"You need more than one room?" asked the old man, eyeing them as he turned back toward them.

"No, one'll be fine," said Bruce. "We're buddies." He grinned wickedly.

The old man shrugged.

141

He didn't seem bothered by them all staying together in the same room. "There's one double and a pull-out couch in the room." He placed the key on the counter. "That'll be fifty-five—in advance—for the first night. How long'll you be stayin'?"

There was a little white number on the key tag. 103. Bruce picked it up. "Do you have anything on the second floor?"

"Nope, sorry," the old man said, shaking his gray head. "We only open the bottom floor this time of year. How long you staying?"

"A day or two," said Bruce. "I guess we'll take the room."

Bruce paid then scooped up the key and they left the office. They walked the short distance across the parking lot until they came to the beige door with the number 103 in large black numbers.

The parking lot was mostly empty. Other than her POS, there were only two other cars in the lot. One was a dark green late-model Chevy, the other a newer yellow Toyota.

Bruce held the door open. A musty scent wafted over Trudy as she entered. The room might be clean, but it hadn't had an airing for some time. A window had to be opened. But first I have to sit down.

Trudy's knees shook when she sat down on one of the two chairs by the window facing the parking lot. A feeling of dread enveloped her. The killer could be waiting for them around any corner. A picture of Emily's bloody corpse flashed through her mind.

Oh, my God...

***

Bruce stared out the motel window at the single streetlight by the side of the highway. The white cone of light shimmered due to the drops of rain falling through its friendly beam. There was no wind, so the rain fell straight to the ground.

He imagined the rain splashing against his bare arms, its coolness, and its fresh feel. He closed his eyes and imagined himself heading down the highway on his bike, the wind whipping through his long hair.

He let go of the thin curtain he'd been holding aside. The room was quiet except for the gentle snoring of Alice, who lay beside Trudy. Trudy's rhythmic breathing made the thin, off-white blanket rise and fall in a steady beat.

Her eyes were closed and he could tell she was dreaming because of the movement under her eyelids.

He couldn't sleep. He was worried. Somewhere out there was a killer, intent on stopping them from getting to the truth, and he wasn't sure he could stop them before one or both of these women were killed.

Trudy seemed oblivious to the danger, and Alice wasn't very bright—she probably hadn't made the connection yet. Trudy was desperate; at least he understood her motivation for seeing this thing through. The cops suspected her and Rocky in Sharon's murder. He didn't think they had killed anyone. Especially that husband. Loser.

Maybe he should've insisted they go to the cops, but he knew the locals or at least the type. He'd encountered small town cops before.

Deputy Summers was an incompetent bastard at the best of times. And the sheriff. He was an oily son of a bitch. Sharon complained about him and his deputy lackey plenty of times. But the sheriff had been out of town when Sharon and Emily died. While he might be a creep, he certainly couldn't have killed them.

The sheriff had once been a homicide pig in Portland, for God's sake. At least that's what he'd told everyone in town, certainly the town council would have checked him out before hiring him.

Who else, then? That was the question. Suspects, he had to find other suspects.

Sanchez seemed focused on Rocky and Trudy, as if they were master criminals or some such bullshit. He shook his head.

He eased one booted foot off the chair he was using as a footrest and shifted his butt. He winced. The damn chairs were so uncomfortable. Stretching his arms over his head, he extended them to work out some of the kinks. Maybe he needed a few minutes shut eye after all.

Glancing at the worn navy blue couch against the wall, he thought about pulling out the bed hidden beneath the overstuffed cushions but decided it would make too much noise. He didn't want to wake the ladies.

"You can pull it out if you want," Trudy said in a low whisper.

"What?" asked Bruce tentatively, glancing at the double bed with its natural pine headboard.

He heard a muffled giggle. "The sofa bed, of course. What did you think I meant?"

He shrugged and his cheeks grew warm. "I—uh—nothing," he said finally. He was glad it was dark in the room so she couldn't see his embarrassment.

"Don't flatter yourself. Now pull out the bed and get some sleep; we've gotta long day ahead of us tomorrow," she said.

"Okay, see you in the mornin'." He went to the couch and managed to pull open the bed hidden inside without making too much noise.

Slipping his feet out of his motorcycle boots, he eased himself under the cool sheets. After placing a lumpy pillow underneath his head, he turned on his side into a fetal position. Within seconds, he slipped into darkness.

* * *

The next morning Bruce was woken by sunlight streaming in through the front window. One of the women had drawn the drapes and was standing there, framed by the sunlight. He blinked and shielded his eyes from the glare.

Eventually the spots coalesced into the familiar shape of blonde Alice, gazing out the window.

"Hey," mumbled Bruce.

"Good morning, sleepyhead," said Alice, glancing at him. "It's almost eight-thirty. Trudy told me to wake you. She's gone to get some coffee and muffins for us so we can hit the rode and go to the shop Sharon used to work at, as soon as it opens."

Bruce nodded and sat up. He placed both hands over his eyes and rubbed the sleep from them. Grunting, he stood and walked into the small bathroom. He needed his morning constitutional before breakfast. A lifetime of habits couldn't be wrong.

Afterward he undressed and climbed into the shower. After testing the water temperature as it rushed through the spigot, he adjusted the taps until he had the perfect balance of cold and hot water, then pulled the silver button on top of the spigot.

He pressed his hands against the shower wall in front of him and leaned toward the wall with his head down and his eyes closed. He thought about Sharon. About when they were kids growing up in Seattle, playing skip on the road with her girlfriends. He thought about beating up kids who bullied her in high school. And the times he'd defended her against their drunken father. This time, though, he had been too late. This time she died.

The hard spray from the showerhead cascaded down on him, running through his long black hair, down his face, around his feet, and finally swirling into the drain.

A sudden wave of regret and grief overcame him. His massive shoulders trembled and tears streamed from his eyes, mingling with the warm water flowing over him. Gulping air, he felt his chest heave with massive sobs and then his whole body began to shake. His sobs echoed off the shower stall's porcelain walls.

He didn't know how long he stood there before there was a knock on the door. He heard a woman's voice asking if he was okay.

"Yeah," he called. There was a muffled reply. He held his breath until the tension in his shoulders eased.

He needed to get a grip. They were in danger and he needed to be strong; the time for grieving would come later.

He turned off the shower.

Pulling back the white plastic shower curtain, he stepped on the thin bathmat into the room full of billowing steam. He removed a large white bath towel from the overhead steel rack that contained three other bath towels and unfolded it. Wrapping his long hair in the towel, he dried it best he could first, then ran the towel over his body until he felt sufficiently dry.

He looked in the mirror after he'd dressed and saw that his eyes were bloodshot and his hair lay flat against his scalp. He fluffed the hair with his long fingers.

After taking a deep breath, he opened the bathroom door and stepped out, leaving the door ajar behind him. A cloud of steam followed him; the window overlooking the parking lot fogged over.

Trudy and Alice sat on opposite sides of the small pine table, talking in low tones, sipping from colorful paper cups; bran muffins on the table rested on white paper napkins.

They didn't seem to notice him until Trudy cast him a brief glance as he sat on the edge of the now neatly made bed and sighed heavily. The two women continued their conversation, ignoring him. They were having a heated debate about some soap opera he had never heard of.

It continually amazed him how people could be so tied up in some stupid, fucked-up TV show. Especially one where the characters had problems that paled when compared with the ones in real life.

"What? Something wrong?" asked Trudy, glancing at him from across the table. Her hands were cupped around a warm white cup with a mist of steam rising over it.

"Nuthin'," he said.

His eyes flicked at her and he caught the crooked smile on her face. Her chestnut brown eyes sparkled in the sunlight that managed to get through the steamed windows, which were beginning to gradually clear.

"I'll bet," she said, easing back in the wood-framed pine chair. "Most guys, not all, don't much like our soaps." She shrugged. "That's okay.

"Want some java?" On the table was a thin cardboard box with an identical paper cup and another muffin. She'd bought for everyone.

"Yeah," he said trying to sound cool, though his stomach growled. He rose from the bed and walked to the table. Inside the box were the cup with a white plastic lid, two creamers, and two packets of white sugar.

He picked up the coffee and the muffin, then walked back to sit on the bed. He began chomping on the muffin between sips of coffee.

"So when do we get started?" he mumbled between mouthfuls.

"Soon as we know which shop we need to go to. I looked in the telephone directory under hair salons and there are at least thirty of them in Newport, scattered across town."

She took a sip from her cup. The warm coffee tasted good on her tongue.

Bruce nodded, then swallowed the last of his muffin. "I know," he paused, placing a fist in front of his mouth to cover a burp. "Sorry."

Trudy smiled. Bruce was certainly polite with his man habits. Rocky would never have bothered covering his mouth or apologizing.

"I think it was a shop named Helen's Beauty Salon," he said. "But I never went there so I don't know exactly where it is."

"You never went to the shop?" asked Trudy. He shrugged a sheepish grin on his face.

She patted his arm while rolling her eyes. "Never mind," she said, "thing is I don't recall seeing a listing for a shop with that name."

Trudy stood and walked to the pine dresser near the bed. The wood-framed mirror, attached to the back of the dresser, reflected her worried expression. She picked up the telephone book she'd laid on it earlier and carried it back to the table, placing it in front of her chair. After sitting down, she opened it.

She flipped the pages until she again found the Barbers and Beauty Salons listings. Using her finger, she scanned the thirty names for Newport. There had to be a lot of hair being updoed, cut, and permed in this small town. The shops had names like Shear Perfection, Happy Hair, or The Cut Above, yet none with a name even close to Helen's Beauty Salon.

"Nope. No Helen's." Shaking her head, she closed the telephone book.

"What now?"

Alice, who'd been concentrating on her tiny bites of muffin, spoke up, "Helen retired."

Trudy and Bruce looked at each other, then together they glared at her.

"What the hell did you say?" asked Bruce before Trudy could speak.

Getting information out of this girl was nearly impossible. Trudy was getting very pissed off.

Alice looked up at him from the remains of her blueberry bran muffin, her eyes wide with fear. "I thought you knew."

Bruce shook his head.

"Well, she did. A year ago. Sharon told me." She looked to Trudy for support. Trudy shook her head. "You guys didn't tell me why we're in Newport," protested Alice.

Trudy's features relaxed and she sighed. "Take it easy, Bruce, she's right. I didn't tell her."

"Fuck," said Bruce, rising from the bed. His butt left an outline on the comforter. He threw his hands in the air. "What do we do now?"

Trudy motioned for him to sit. He did so, his dark eyes glared at Alice, who avoided looking at him.

"Alice," she said softly, "did Sharon ever mention the name of the new salon owner?"

Alice kept her blue eyes focused on the remains of the muffin. "Other than calling her the old bitch, no, not really."

Trudy rolled her eyes. "I need you to concentrate, Alice."

Trudy reached over, placed two fingers underneath the younger woman's chin, and pulled her head up. Blue watery eyes locked with Trudy's. "Did Sharon ever speak of a friend? Someone she liked to hang out with in Newport. A girlfriend. Someone like you and Emily?"

Alice's expression brightened. She nodded. "Yeah. Fred," she said.

"Fred?" Trudy said as she glanced at Bruce, who shrugged. "Who's Fred?"

"A girl she worked with at the salon."

Trudy nodded to Bruce. Now they were getting somewhere. They would find this girl and see if she could help them identify who belonged to those initials listed in Sharon's phone book.

"What's Fred's last name?"

"I dunno," said Alice, shrugging her narrow shoulders. "Maybe the shop was sold and it's still a salon, but under another name?"

Trudy nodded. Helen retired. It made perfect sense. Why hadn't she thought of it? Maybe Alice wasn't such a dumb blonde after all.

"Okay, let's hit every shop until we find this Fred." Trudy opened the telephone book and ripped out the page with the salon names. She picked up her purse off the dresser, along with her car keys.

Bruce had the room key. Once outside in the parking lot, they walked to the car and got in, with Trudy behind the wheel, Alice in the back seat, Bruce beside Trudy, crammed into the passenger seat. Bruce knew the town better than she did, but she felt like driving today. She handed the listings page to him. "Call out when we need to turn," she said.

"Ya know we coulda phoned the salons and asked for Fred," whispered Bruce under his breath.

'Yeah, we could do that, but I suspect she'd run for parts unknown if she knew we were coming," Trudy said.

Bruce nodded appreciatively.

The engine turned over after one turn of the key and seemed to be running better. They were no closer to Sharon's murderer, but Trudy thought today just might be the turning point.

Nineteen

AFTER AN HOUR OF TRYING A FEW DIFFERENT SHOPS without success, they stopped in front of a hair shop situated in a group of four storefronts bordering the coast highway with the name Happy Hair in large, red, block letters on a backlit sign above the front picture window. Through the window, Trudy saw two women standing behind black barber chairs, chatting amiably with two men as they cut their hair. The men looked interested in the conversation.

With the buxom, Barbie Doll look of the two hair stylists, she could understand why. She hoped one of them was Fred, though neither of them looked like a Fred to her.

Bruce opened the door of the shop, causing a tiny bell over the door to tinkle brightly. One of the women turned to look at them. "We'll be with you shortly. Please have a seat," she said, giving them a toothpaste smile. Trudy smiled thinly and nodded. Alice took a seat in the row of shiny, black, plastic chairs next to the door, picked up a woman's fashion magazine, and began to flip through the pages.

Bruce sat next to her. Trudy sat as well, crossing her legs and holding her purse in her lap.

She glanced at Bruce and saw he was studying the two hairdressers. From the look in his eyes, he liked what he saw. She smiled to herself and began to study the shop's layout.

It had three cutting chairs on both sides of the shop floor, each in front of a workstation. The shop smelled of lemon floor cleaner. It was still early. No doubt later in the day, the air in here would smell like a chemical factory from the perm solutions favored by most hair shop owners.

An arch separated the cutting area from the sinks for washing hair, the perm chairs, and the dryers. Beyond that was a wooden office door, which was closed at the moment. Maybe there was someone else in the office?

One of the customers laughed, breaking her train of thought. Barbie Number One—the one nearest to Trudy, Alice, and Bruce—removed the protective apron that covered the client's street clothes and the white paper sanex strip from the man's neck.

He continued to chuckle and smile at Barbie Number One as he followed her to the reception counter, set against the opposite wall. He paid his bill with a wink at the girl, and the bell over the door tinkled again as he went outside.

Barbie Number One placed the money in a hidden cash drawer and then stuffed the five-dollar tip between her Pamela-Anderson-size breasts.

She looked at the trio, casting them the same phony smile as before. Her blue eyes sparkled when she spoke. "Haircut?" she asked, eyeing Bruce.

Trudy thought for a moment he was going to say yes; before he spoke, she'd better break up this little sex fest. Sorry to disappoint you, big guy. "Hi, I'm Trudy Wilson. Is there a Fred here?"

The smile on Barbie Number One's face wavered slightly and her eyes flicked to Barbie Number Two, who was sweeping the hair from around the cutting chairs.

"Who?" asked Barbie Number Two, her red nail-polish-tipped fingers gripping the broom handle so tightly her knuckles turned white. Trudy was certain if she gripped the broom any tighter, it would snap like a toothpick.

"Fred," repeated Trudy. "We're looking for Fred." Trudy continued, hoping to rattle the two Barbie's. "We're looking for a hairdresser named Fred or Fredericka, something like that. Sorry, we don't have a last name. We thought you might be able to help us because the hairdresser worked here for the previous owner."

Barbie Number Two stared at her, her eyes unblinking. She shook her head. "No, I'm afraid I don't know anyone by that name." She glanced over at her partner, who had her head down, playing with the combs on her station, seemingly oblivious to the conversation. "Liz, what about you?"

Liz shook her head.

"Sorry. It looks like you've reached a dead end." She smiled brightly, her eyes dancing again. "Will there be anything else we can do for you?"

"No, thanks," said Trudy, standing. Bruce and Alice joined her and together they walked outside.

After the door closed behind them, Trudy stopped and turned to Bruce. "We need a coffee," she said, pointing to the coffee shop across the street with the predictable name of Mom's painted in frosted white lettering on the front window.

Bruce nodded; a crooked smile graced his ruddy face. They would be able to keep an eye on the Barbie's from there.

The traffic cleared enough so they could run across the street, though a green Dodge pickup honked at them as they ran. He was clearly speeding, but seemed to think they were in the wrong anyway.

Bruce gave the guy the one-fingered salute. The driver slowed to glare at the big man, but realizing Bruce could flatten him with one hand tied behind his back, sped up and disappeared down the highway.

Bruce turned to Trudy, who scowled at him. "That was uncalled for," she said.

Bruce shrugged. "Son of a bitch deserved it."

They entered the diner through the glass door. Closing the door behind them, they were met by the heady smells of a mixture of bacon, eggs, and coffee. Perhaps a real breakfast might improve our mood, thought Trudy. They'd been pushing themselves pretty hard.

There wasn't a sign telling them to wait to be seated, so they sat in one of the booths overlooking the street. They could watch Happy Hair from here. There was something about the two Barbie's' reactions that bothered Trudy. They lied, she concluded, but why?

A blonde waitress wearing a pale yellow uniform with white apron tied around her waist approached the table. She held a pale green order pad in one hand and a pen in the other. She smiled warmly and her pale peach lipstick shone in the stray sunlight coming through the front window. A nametag over her left breast identified her as Peggy.

Trudy smiled in return.

"What can I get you folks?" asked the waitress, holding her pad at the ready.

"We'll start with some coffees all round," said Trudy. "Can we see menus?"

The woman used her pen as a pointer and indicated a blackboard, hanging over the red linoleum lunch counter with its shiny, red-cushioned stools. Trudy dug in her purse for her eyeglasses case. Damn, I'm getting old.

Bruce's eyebrows arched. Trudy shrugged, opened the case, and pulled out the wire-framed glasses. She put them on and began reading the board. "I'll have the $2.95 special: two eggs over easy, rye toast, and hash browns," said Trudy, pulling off her glasses and putting them away.

"Same," said Bruce.

"Just white toast and jam for me," said Alice, her attention out the front window, gazing at the stream of traffic passing by. There was a constant hum of tires on pavement coming through the large, single pane window.

The waitress disappeared and soon came back with three cups of coffee on white saucers. She placed one cup of the hot coffee in front of each of them.

"Excuse me, Peggy," said Trudy, a smile in her voice. "Do you know the hair shop across the street?"

Peggy's eyes flitted to Happy Hair across the highway then back at Trudy. "Yeah. If you mean Helen's old place."

Trudy nodded. Bruce leaned forward, resting his arms on the red linoleum surface of the table. The cushions squeaked.

"There's a new owner," Peggy explained. "Helen retired and moved away. I don't know the new owner, but it's hard to miss those two working there." She grunted.

Bruce grinned.

Trudy gave him a withering look then said, "How well did you know Helen?"

"She came in her just about every day," said Peggy. "She and her employees used to come in every morning together for coffee. Helen always paid. She was real good to the people who worked for her. Small town. You know how it is."

Trudy felt a twinge inside. Yeah, she knew all about small towns.

"Did you ever meet someone named Sharon Carstairs?"

Peggy nodded. "Yeah, sure. Good gal was here a while before… you know." Peggy looked around, then lowered her voice to a whisper. "Small towns are full of gossip and I don't know you people, so maybe I shouldn't say any more."

"Sharon's dead," said Bruce flatly, his dark eyes fixed on Peggy's.

Her eyes went wide and her body began to tremble. "What? Oh, my God." Her pale hazel eyes brimmed with tears.

"I'm her brother," said Bruce. "We think she's been murdered."

Trudy could see the shock flow across Peggy's features and her face drained of color. Trudy stood and helped Peggy sit on the cushioned bench seat next to her. They waited while Peggy absorbed the news.

"I didn't know," she said, her voice rife with apology.

Bruce shook his head. "The cops thought it was an accident at first. Then they thought it might be Trudy here." He nodded toward Trudy. "Or her husband."

"How well did you know my sister?"

"Hummm. Well. Okay, I guess we used to go out to the bars together once in a while." She blushed, then her moist eyes drifted to meet Bruce's. "She was a little… wild."

Bruce grimaced. "Yeah, she was—a little."

A thin smile crossed Peggy's lips. "She had a lot of boyfriends."

"So we heard," said Trudy. She reached over and rested one hand on Peggy's. "We have Sharon's black book. Unfortunately, she had a code for recording the names of her boyfriends. She only wrote their initials. Would you be able to decipher them?"

"Maybe," said Peggy, nodding.

"I think one of the blondes is leaving," said Alice, pointing toward Happy Hair across the street.

Trudy looked out the window, and sure enough, one of the Barbie's was outside, dressed in a thigh-length blue coat, her hands buried in the pockets. There was no smile on her face now. Instead, her features were a mask of anxious energy, her eyes flitting back and forth, covering the street. She failed to see them watching her. She turned and started walking to one end of the building.

"That's Liz," said Bruce.

"How do you know?" asked Trudy.

He eyed her with a slight grin on his lips. "I know, okay?"

Trudy nodded. Yeah, right.

"Maybe you and I can follow her while Alice stays here to show the black book to Peggy?"

Bruce glanced at Alice, who nodded sheepishly. She wasn't into the detective thing anyway.

"Yeah, let's go," Trudy, said.

Peggy slid off the bench to stand next to the table while Bruce and Trudy slid out after her. Reaching for their jackets where they'd hung them, Trudy pulled a ten-dollar bill from her purse and placed it on the table. "Peggy, that's for your help. Keep the coffee warm. We'll be back."

Peggy slid into the bench seat across from Alice. Trudy slipped the black book from inside the pocket of her jacket and laid it on the table.

"You keep good care of this, okay?' she said to Alice in a low, serious voice.

Alice nodded.

Bruce and Trudy rushed across the room to the front door. After slamming the door behind them, they darted across the street. Bruce held his large hands up to stop traffic and this time no one complained.

"Where did she go?" asked Trudy breathlessly.

"That way," said Bruce, pointing to the corner of the block where a side street created an intersection. They rushed to the corner of the building in time to see a blue pickup truck pulling away. Trudy's heart beat hard in her chest. Rocky?

She managed to see the license number of the truck. It wasn't Rocky's, but it sure looked like his truck. Relief washed over her.

Trudy could clearly see the Barbie's blonde head and her blue jacket in the passenger's seat through the truck's rear window. Her head was turned toward the driver. All Trudy could make out about the driver was a man with dark, curly hair. Then they were gone. The truck disappeared around a corner into a side road.

Trudy stared after the truck. Her eyes burned with intensity.

Bruce watched the truck disappear, a look of disgust on his face. "Damn it! We lost her!" He looked at Trudy, his hands raised in frustration. He froze upon seeing the puzzlement in her eyes. "Am I missing something?"

"I've seen that truck before," she said flatly. "Outside Sharon's house the night she died. And you know what's really interesting?"

Bruce shook his head, clearly not understanding what she was getting at.

"It looks exactly like Rocky's truck."

It was almost as if someone were trying to frame her husband. She gritted her teeth.

And that really made her mad.

Twenty

Sheriff John Miller was a rugged man with piercing blue eyes like those Paul Newman had been blessed with. He was trim and lean for a man nearing his mid fifties. His tan uniform shirt had the razor thin line that comes from expert ironing.

His dark curls were tinged with gray, but his swarthy, world-weary features belied his true age. The man should have been a male model, thought Dolores, studying the man after entering his office.

He stood and smiled when she entered. Laugh lines appeared around the edges of his dancing blue eyes. He was a real charmer. Her mother would call him an old smoothie.

Sanchez held out her right hand.

He grasped the offered hand in his. His dry, warm flesh was rough, but he applied just the right pressure. Small-town sheriffs were often diplomats as well as peace officers.

She smiled. "Nice to meet you, Sheriff."

"Call me John, please," he said, releasing her hand and hooking his thumbs on his black leather gun belt.

The holster contained a nine-millimeter Glock automatic, safely held in place by the buttoned-down strap running around the trigger guard so no one could take it from him without a struggle.

In his left breast pocket hung a pair of dark sunglasses and a single, gold plated pen clipped to the inside of the pocket. The guy loves his uniform, thought Sanchez. He's clearly a perfectionist.

"Of course, John," she said. "Call me Dolores."

He nodded, then they each took a seat, the desk between them. Sanchez glanced around the room. "Nice office."

Nodding, he got immediately down to business. "How is your investigation going?"

He leaned forward in his chair and interlocked his fingers in his lap. "I'd also like to know why the State Police became involved in this investigation. I do have experience with homicide, you know." He gazed into her eyes, his face impassive, but she could clearly see the anger behind them.

"You were out of town and my boss thought we might be able to help." She shrugged. "There hasn't been a murder in Fairview in more than twenty years. And you don't have the facilities. The station is like a fifties museum of police work, don't you think?" She grinned.

Miller eased back in his chair and laughed. "Yeah. You're right, of course. I came here for the peace and quiet. Any help you can offer will be very much appreciated. How about I make us some coffee?"

"Yeah, sure," said Sanchez.

She followed him into the main office, where the coffeemaker rested on top of a three-drawer filing cabinet to the left of Miller's desk. The sheriff had his back to her while he made the coffee. She looked back toward his office.

She'd noticed the walls were dotted with certificates for service, shooting medals set in black frames, and pictures of a much younger sheriff in his Portland Police uniform. In one, he stood in a line of similarly dressed cops.

There were no personal pictures on the walls or on his desk.

Miller glanced back at her as he spooned dark coffee grounds into the filter. "Those are pictures from my Portland days. Haven't had time to put up my Fairview ones yet," he explained.

Odd, she thought, I didn't say anything, yet he noticed me looking. Once a detective always a detective.

He held the empty glass pot by its black plastic handle. "I'll be right back. I gotta get some water."

Nodding, she watched him until he disappeared into the men's room down a short hallway.

She walked across the office until she was standing outside his open office door. She studied one of the pictures on the wall behind his desk. In it, the sheriff, in his Portland PD dress uniform, was receiving a medal from a distinguished older man dressed in an expensive suit. Must be the Portland chief, she concluded.

"My retirement photo." Miller's voice from behind her startled her. She went in and sat down in his office.

"The chief loved ceremony," Miller continued. "That was my long service award. Twenty-five years on the force." Miller filled the reservoir of the machine with water from the glass carafe. Sanchez detected a trace of bitterness underlying his words.

Raising his eyes to hers, he offered a thin-lipped smile, but his eyes remained hard, as if they were filled with ice. She called the look "dead eyes." She'd seen eyes like the sheriff's on a lot of cops and many suspects.

In her limited experience, more cops had dead eyes than any other strata of society. The ability to bury your emotions was one of the hazards of the job. It made normal relationships difficult.

He finished pouring the water and set the carafe under the spout, then flicked the on switch.

Crossing her legs, she placed her arms on the arms of the chair. Her posture sent the signal she was open but still cautious. Body language said so much, and very few people ever realize the signals they were sending by how they sat or walked or carried themselves. It was something she had practiced.

Sheriff Miller sat down in the chair behind his desk. In the silence, the coffeemaker spat and soon coffee began to flow into the glass carafe. The room began to smell of brewing coffee.

"Don't you love that smell?" asked Miller, a crooked grin on his tanned features. His blue eyes now shone through her like blue searchlights.

She smiled, then casually folded her hands on the lap of her gray pantsuit and leaned back in the chair. "Have you read the reports about Sharon Carstairs and Emily Cross?" she asked.

He leaned back in his chair, one hand on his right leg; the other lay flat on the desk, playing with his blue metallic ballpoint pen that he'd picked up from where it lay next to a plastic-covered green blotter. His eyes were focused on the pen as if he'd never seen one before. "Yeah, I read 'em."

"Any conclusions?" she asked, keeping her eyes on his tanned face. His eyes never drifted from the pen.

He shrugged. "I'd say the two events aren't connected."

"I'd say otherwise. I think they're definitely connected."

A twisted smile crossed his lips and he glanced up from the pen to gaze into her brown eyes.

A dimple appeared on his right cheek and she sensed his considerable charisma directed at her. Mentally she shook off the feeling. This guy was the sheriff and she didn't trust him. Yet.

Sighing heavily, he leaned forward to rest his weight on his arms with the pen now gripped in the fingers of his right hand.

"Detective," he began.

The tolerance in his voice irked her. Another dick that thinks female cops are only pc ornaments. Now he was pissing her off, his first mistake.

"I've been a cop longer than you've been outta diapers, so I know what the hell I'm talking about. I was a homicide dick in Portland for fifteen years. I've seen a lotta death. The Carstairs woman's death smells like suicide, in my professional opinion."

He flipped open the manila file folder in front of him to the picture of Sharon. It was one from her house—the one with her and her brother standing in front of a Christmas tree. They each had one arm around the other's waist, smiling into the camera. Sharon's streaked-blonde good looks and ample bosom gave her the appearance of the ideal California beach bunny.

"And this one," Miller said, as he turned over Sharon's picture to one of a dark-eyed brunette, lying in a pool of her own blood, her high cheekbones pale, her eyes focused on eternity. "She was murdered. That's the one we need to concentrate on."

"Okay," said Sanchez, deciding she wasn't going to argue the point until they received the transcripts on the answering machine tapes from the state lab. "Let me brief you on what I've come up with so far, then we can decide together on next steps. Okay?"

Miller nodded slowly. The look in his eye reminded her she was a consultant only. The sheriff wanted the lead.

The coffeemaker had stopped spitting. He stood and grabbed two white mugs from where they sat next to the coffeemaker and poured two cups of the streaming coffee.

"Just milk," said Sanchez.

"All I got's whitener."

She nodded and he put one spoon of the white powder in each cup, and one spoon of brown sugar from a plain glass bowl in his mug.

He carried the cups to the desk, placing one in front of her. She nodded, then continued. "Deputy Summers and I interviewed every person on the block near the house where the victim was found. No one reported hearing or seeing anything unusual. They reported no unusual sounds or strange vehicles in the area just prior to the murder."

"Who called it in?" asked the sheriff.

"An unidentified woman. She refused to give her name."

His only response was a nod. The corners of his mouth curled up slightly. He took a sip from his cup to cover his mouth.

She continued. "We cordoned off the site as soon as we arrived. The lab boys from Portland should be here by morning. They'll fine-tooth comb the site for clues. We did find tire tracks in the soft dirt at the edge the driveway that may provide us something. The lab boys are pretty good."

Miller had hands cupped around his mug, gazing at the floor as he listened. Intermittently he blew away the steam rising from the coffee.

"Murder weapon?" he asked.

"Summers and I searched the area as best we could. Negative on a weapon before we lost the light. First thing in the morning, we're going to search outside our cordoned off area.

"Hopefully we'll get lucky and find it, but I'm not confident."

Miller nodded again, sipped at his coffee, and swallowed. "Anything else?"

"Yeah. When Summers arrived on the scene there was a biker named…" She pulled her notebook from her inside suit pocket, flipping it to the page where she'd made her notes. "…Bruce Carstairs, with the hairdresser. Summers found them near the body."

Miller's eyebrows arched. He flipped back the picture of Sharon and then gazed into Sanchez's eyes. "Wasn't her name, Carstairs?" he asked, pressing his right index finger in the center of Sharon's picture.

"Yeah, but we interviewed him and Mrs. Wilson, and searched them and their car. We have no reason to suspect they were involved."

"Why not?"

"Well, for one thing, Wilson didn't know the vic and had only been to the house once before. Carstairs had the vic's blood on him, but not enough to be the killer." She shook her head. "No way. If he'd cut her throat, it'd be like he'd bathed in the stuff. And he had very recently become the vic's lover. I phoned the names in to my office and both came back clean before I let them go. She couldn't possibly have the strength to make the killing blow and he seemed genuinely upset by the vic's death. It didn't feel right."

He nodded and a small grin crossed his face. "Not bad, Detective, but they must've been involved somehow. I think you should pick them both up for further questioning. And this time," he swiveled his chair to face her. "Why don't you leave the questioning of suspects to an old pro who knows what he's doing?" He winked at her.

She fumed inside but smiled thinly to cover her disgust. I'm gonna kick this slimy son of a bitch's butt, but not now. Now I need him to put this one in the record book. No wonder he's not with Portland PD anymore.

***

Sheriff John Miller sat in his office, watching Sanchez through the window behind his desk. She got into her car, started it, then drove off to mingle with the highway traffic.

"Kelly!" Miller called to Deputy Summers, who had just returned from patrol and now sat at his desk just outside the sheriff's office. "Get your ass in here. We need to talk."

Summers nodded. Hitching his right thumb in his leather gun belt, he sauntered into the sheriff's office, closing the door with his right foot. He sat in one of two green chairs in front of the sheriff's desk and waited. Miller had his back to Summers, the back of the leather chair like a wall of tarpaper separating them. His boss seemed to be studying the photos lined up across the wall.

He swallowed hard when he realized this wasn't a social call. Something was up. His instincts screamed that the something had to do with the bitch from the State Police who'd just left the office.

Miller spun his chair around slowly until he faced Summers with his arms resting on the arms of the executive chair. The room was still, the air suddenly as heavy as a Louisiana summer. The smell of sweat drifted into his nostrils. Millers blue eyes drilled into his soul.

John Miller's expression was flat, cold, and calculating. In his experience with the man, Summers knew this wasn't a good sign.

"Kelly, do you recall us speaking about that piece of shit biker named Carstairs, and that stupid bitch hairdresser, Trudy Wilson?" His tone sent shivers down Summers spine.

"Yeah, sure, I…"

Miller shook his head, so Summers stopped speaking.

"Where are they?"

"I dunno. Exactly," said Summers, his voice trembling slightly.

Miler's eyebrows went up. "Exactly?"

"Well, they left together in her car. Carstairs bike is still at the motel he's staying at so I assumed…"

"What's the first rule of police work?" asked Miller, frowning.

"Never assume?"

Miller nodded, his face a mask of grim humor. "Sanchez has left to find them. I want you to find them first. Let me know when you do. Understood?"

Summers nodded, then rose to his feet and turned to leave.

"And Kelly. Don't fuck up this time, okay? I don't need some smart-ass state police detective showing us up on this, do I?"

Summers shook his head and walked quickly to his desk to retrieve his uniform hat. He was out the front door, slamming it behind him, in seconds.

Miller watched him go, smiling to himself when the door slammed shut. He leaned back in his high-backed leather chair and scanned the pictures on the wall until his blue eyes fell on the photo of him receiving his twenty-five year plaque from the Portland chief.

He would show them—show them all. His eyes narrowed to fine slits and he steepled his fingers in front of him as he eased back in the chair, causing it to creak in the silence. The coffeemaker bubbled once, then silence returned.

Twenty-One

THEY WALKED SILENTLY BACK TOWARD THE DINER. Trudy's lips were thin, her eyes filled with hate and her face red. Bruce glanced at her out of the corner of one eye as he walked beside her. The little bell over the door on Mom's Diner rang brightly as they entered.

Alice looked up as they approached the booth, Trudy in the lead. She was smiling until she saw Trudy's grim expression, then the smile quickly faded. She cast her eyes down to the page of the black book Peggy and she had been reading.

Trudy sat down across from the two women and gazed out the front window, her eyes hard, her arms crossed.

"We lost her," said Bruce, matter-of-factly. He joined Trudy, across from Alice and Peggy.

Peggy looked up from the page. "I think I might be able to help."

Trudy cleared her throat and Bruce leaned forward.

"I know several of these initials. Some are for girls who worked with Sharon. One is Helen's old phone number, and some are phone numbers in different towns up and down the coast. I know because the area codes and the first three numbers aren't from Newport.

For sure one is a number in Fairview, which might be the one you're looking for."

"Do you know whose it might be?" asked Bruce.

Peggy shook her head. "No." She paused and looked like she was trying to squeeze out some memory to help her recognize the initials next to the telephone numbers. Her face squished as if she was sucking on a lemon and her eyes were now shut tight. "LB?" she asked, her voice low, barely above a whisper.

Her eyes popped open and she shook her head. "Nope. I can't think of anyone with those initials."

Alice cast her eyes at the table and she had a sheepish expression on her face. Her high cheeks were red. "I think I might know who those initials stand for now that I see them."

Bruce stared at the young woman, his eyes flashing with unconcealed anger. "Why the fuck didn't you say so before?"

Trudy put one hand on his shoulder. "Now, Bruce, don't be too hard on the girl. She's been through a lot lately."

"Well, so have I," said Bruce, his brow creased. He sat back against the wall of red vinyl and crossed his arms over his massive chest, the veins appearing on his heavily muscled forearms.

"I know," said Trudy, trying to soothe her tormented friend. Everyone was in pain right now. Their emotions were going to boil over if they didn't get answers soon.

Trudy turned to look at Alice, who stared at Bruce, her eyes brimming with fear. A thought crossed Trudy's mind. She shouldn't be that afraid. Her eyes narrowed.

"Alice, is there something you're not telling us?"

"I don't know what you mean." Alice shrugged, keeping her watery eyes fixed on the large man glaring at her. "All I know is LB is a code Sharon used for the guy she'd been seeing in Fairview."

"What does it mean?" asked Trudy, her trembling voice betrayed her impatience. Alice was hiding something. She was afraid, but not of Bruce.

"Love Bunny," said Alice, without a hint of humor to her voice.

Trudy glanced at Bruce. His face was flushed. Turning back to look at the girl, she smiled as sweetly as possible. Leaning forward until her elbows rested on the table, she locked her fingers in front of her.

"Now, Alice, I can see you're frightened of something or someone, but you need to tell us all you know about this boyfriend of Sharon's. What's his name?"

Alice looked at her like a deer in the lights of an eighteen-wheeler that knew it was about to become venison hamburger. "I don't know his name. I never met him. They'd meet late, then she'd be out all night. She came home in time to shower, change clothes, then go to work."

She paused to think, her forehead wrinkled with the effort. "I did see him pick her up once. He was driving a blue truck of some kind." She shrugged. "I don't know much about trucks, or cars for that matter, so I don't know what kind it was."

"Would you know the truck if you saw it again?" asked Trudy, her lips forming a wide smile. She studied the younger woman's face, trying to decide if she was telling the truth.

"Yeah, maybe," said Alice.

"Let's get outta here," said Bruce.

"Is there anything else I can do?" asked Peggy, watching as they left the booth and walked across the diner toward the front door.

Trudy glanced at the middle-aged waitress in her pale yellow uniform. "I'd suggest if anyone asks, you tell them you never saw us."

"Why?" asked Peggy.

"Because the last person who could've provided us information is dead."

Trudy followed Bruce and Alice out the door. It rattled as it closed behind them.

The wind had picked up and the air reeked of seawater. Overhead, seagulls called to each other as they headed inland away from the ocean. A storm was coming.

Trudy grabbed Bruce's arm to hold him back. "You go ahead, Alice. I need a quick word with Bruce." Alice shrugged and got in the back seat of the car.

Bruce looked at her quizzically one eyebrow arched. "Bruce, I suspect Alice is playing a game with us. She's trying to deceive us." Bruce opened his mouth to speak but Trudy spoke first. "Before you ask no, I don't know why. Not yet. I suggest we play along until she makes a mistake. You with me?"

"Yeah, of course." It felt good to know a man trusted you again.

Trudy wrapped one arm around Bruce's and they started toward the car. Trudy turned her head to steal a peek of Peggy, still seated in the booth staring at them, her mouth hanging open, her face pale as new snow. Trudy felt a twinge of regret at scaring the poor woman, but it was for her own safety.

Soon they were seated in the front seats of the car with Bruce driving this time. He turned the key in the ignition. The little motor shook the whole car as the engine tried to turn until finally, with a stutter, it caught, and Bruce pressed down hard on the gas pedal. The engine roared until he eased back, then it began to shudder and spurt as it ran on.

Gradually it smoothed out enough that he was able to shift into drive, then steer into the traffic headed north on the coast highway.

He glared at the road as the rain began to fall and flicked the lever that turned on the windshield wipers.

The wipers were slow and didn't give much coverage, so seeing the road ahead was a challenge.

"Sorry," said Alice from the back seat behind Trudy, who was in the passenger seat next to Bruce.

"Save it," said Bruce. "Bitch," he added in a low whisper, causing Trudy to glare at him. He shrugged when he noticed her expression.

"Have you thought to try phoning the number in Sharon's book for LB?" asked Alice.

"Of course," said Trudy, casting a knowing glance at Bruce.

He remained silent, keeping his eyes focused on the road. He glanced back at Trudy from the corner of one eye and nodded. His dark eyes twinkled.

"Good," said Alice.

Trudy knew they had fooled the girl. She thought they were going to follow another wild goose chase. The number had to be a fake or out of service. It only made sense. Alice couldn't be trusted. Anything she said was suspect.

The trio drove the rest of way back to Fairview in stony silence.

***

Sanchez checked at Trudy's hair shop first. There was a hand-written sign taped to the front door with the words "On Vacation" written in black felt pen.

Next she tried the restaurant where Alice worked. The owner said she'd fired her when some broad and a big biker guy came in and took her away.

She then drove to the Wilson's house and found Rocky. He answered the door in stained boxers and an undershirt. He had a can of beer in one hand and obviously hadn't shaved, evidenced by the gray stubble on his face. His bloodshot eyes and stale-beer-and-cigarette breath meant he'd been on a bender.

She left Trudy's house, going to Bruce's motel. Still no luck.

After pulling her white, unmarked car over to the side of the highway, she used her cell phone to call her captain in Portland.

After two rings, the Captain picked up. "Schultz."

"Captain. It's Sanchez, sir," she said.

"Sanchez. Hope you're having a nice vacation." He paused. "So, you got that case wrapped up?" He sounded impatient.

"Not exactly, sir."

"What's the problem?"

She had his attention. He was a good cop and about as professional as they came. And a damn good boss. He would find a way to help her, whatever it took.

"Well, sir, it's the Fairview sheriff. There's something not right about him. My sixth sense is screaming at me."

Schultz chuckled. "Let me guess: sexist pig, right?"

"Yeah, sir. But that's only part of the story. I think the guy's trying to set me up."

"What do you mean?" His voice became serious.

"He wants me to arrest two people for murder who couldn't possibly have done it. I know I'm kinda new to the detective job, but I just know these two are innocent. One is the brother of vic one, and from what I know of him, he was the lover of the second vic." She heard a deep sigh on the other end of the line. She knew this was sounding like one of those cheesy daytime soaps her mom watched, but she continued.

"It just doesn't make sense. And the other is a middle aged hairdresser who couldn't physically have killed either of the victims."

"Want me to check the whole lot of 'em out and get back to you?"

"Yes, sir," she said, her voice edged with determination.

There was a short pause as she heard paper rustle. "Okay, give me the names and DOB's, if you've got 'em."

She gave him the information, including what she knew of Sheriff Miller's background. She waited while he finished writing it all down.

"Okay, Sanchez, you keep looking for the woman and the biker, and I'll run this information and get back you. I'll call you later tonight. Okay?"

"Thank you, sir," she said. She glanced at her watch. It was about three thirty in the afternoon.

"You're welcome, Detective. After all, what are commanding officers for?" An edge of humor crept into his voice.

"Yes, sir," she said as she flipped her cell phone closed. He was a good guy and a great cop. Until now, she hadn't thought he even liked her. She would have to reappraise her relationship with her boss. Nice guy, with a good sense of humor, and one of the smartest men on the planet. He was too old for her to be romantically involved, but she thought someone like him was the man for her. Leaning her head back against the headrest, she sighed and closed her eyes. Maybe by the time this day was over, she would have the answers she was after.

She was reminded of something her police academy instructor used to say: be careful what you wish for, you just might get it.

Twenty-Two

BRUCE PULLED INTO THE PARKING LOT OF THE HILLTOP just after four in the afternoon. Too early for dinner, but Trudy suggested they stop for a bite before heading to their respective homes.

The sky had become so dark, Bruce had had to turn on the car's headlights. The little wipers weren't doing much to clear the rain off the windshield.

Once parked, they shielded themselves with their jackets as they rushed from the car into the restaurant. Bruce pushed the door in and held it open to allow Trudy and Alice to enter the customer waiting area ahead of him.

Inside, the same manager from their earlier visit greeted them. Trudy wondered if the guy had a home.

Her stomach growled, making her realize they'd never actually eaten anything at Mom's Diner in Newport. The talk with Peggy had taken priority. A good thing, too, thought Trudy. We might even get to the bottom of this mess yet.

They followed the manager to a table with a view of the kitchen and the two tanned Hispanic cooks in their white paper hats, white uniform shirts, and thin dark mustaches.

The odors from the kitchen made Trudy even hungrier and her mouth began to water.

They were seated in a booth far enough from other customers that they wouldn't be overheard. The manager placed three plastic-coated menus on the table, then left to get the glasses of ice water Alice requested.

They sat in awkward silence until the manager had come and gone again. They ordered food this time: Alice a chicken Caesar, Bruce a cheeseburger with fries, and Trudy a turkey sandwich with a salad instead of fries.

As impossible as it seemed, the rain had begun to fall more heavily outside. They watched it dance off the pavement and bounce off the cars. After what seemed like an eternity, it finally it began to wane and the cloud cover began to lighten, though it continued to rain.

"Shitty weather," said Trudy.

"What the fuck do I look like? The fuckin' weatherman?" asked Bruce. One of the gray-haired ladies a few tables away glanced in their direction, a look of disgust on her sallow features. She obviously didn't appreciate Bruce's language.

Trudy had to admit he was a bit loud. "Bruce, give it a rest, will you?" asked Trudy. "Or at least lower your voice." She understood his anger. Alice could have done more to help his sister. And she'd been lying to them sending them all over the countryside to find nothing. Trudy had the urge to pop her one herself, but they had to let her make a mistake so they could find out who she was protecting.

So for now it was a hands off policy toward Alice.

"Sorry. I'm pissed is all," he lowered his voice to a harsh whisper. "With her."

"I know. I'm not too happy myself, but she is the only lead we have right now."

"Hey, I'm right here, you know," said Alice with an air of indignation.

Trudy glared at her. "Little miss, don't push me too far. I've a mind to let the big guy here take out his frustration on you. And somehow I don't think he'll be too nice about it, get it?"

Alice nodded, her eyes wide with fear.

A noise on the highway caught Trudy's attention. It was a large white car with a single occupant, entering the parking lot. The car pulled up in front of the restaurant, stopped, and the driver's door swung open. Trudy recognized Detective Sanchez.

"Oh, shit," she said under her breath.

Just then their food arrived—the manager delivered it himself.

Bruce followed Trudy's line of sight, the color draining from his cheeks when he spotted the cop headed their way. He glanced at Trudy and she shook her head. They had nowhere to hide and not enough time to run. Bruce slumped lower in his seat.

After placing a plate of food in front of each of them and a bottle of ketchup on the table, the manager asked, "Is there anything else I can get you?"

"Not right now," said Trudy. "Maybe later."

He nodded, then walked away, shaking his head.

Sanchez walked through the front door into the lobby, where the manager greeted her. She seemed to ask him a question. He nodded toward their table and the detective headed toward them.

When she reached the booth, she slid onto the brown, vinyl-covered seat next to Bruce, placing her hands flat on the table. Her dark eyes were deadly serious.

"I've been looking for you two," she said, her voice low.

Trudy stomach was suddenly in knots. Her hunger had just evaporated.

***

Trudy stared at Dolores Sanchez, her mouth open. "You believe us?" she asked, hardly believing what she was hearing.

"Yeah. I think so," said Sanchez, her dark eyes hard, a frown creasing her forehead.

Alice avoided eye contact by looking down at the table.

"What's with your friend?" asked Sanchez, nodding at Alice.

"Bitch has been lying to us since we left Fairview," said Bruce, his bitterness clear in his tone.

"What do you mean?"

Bruce reached underneath the table, grabbed the cloth bag containing his sister's black book, and threw it on the table.

"What's this?" asked Sanchez, her eyebrows arching in surprise.

"My sisters diary," said Bruce. He glanced at Trudy, who rolled her eyes and sighed.

Sanchez frowned. "Withholding important evidence from the police in the course of an investigation is a crime, don't you know?"

"Wha…" said Bruce. "Uh—I didn't think…" He closed his mouth. He'd dug them a big enough hole. They might be going to jail after all.

Just then the manager appeared with a coffeepot. "Is there anything else I can get for you?"

Seeing the untouched food, he frowned. "Is something wrong?"

"Nothing a little truth and apple pie might fix," said Sanchez, glaring at Trudy and Bruce. Sanchez turned to face the manager, who now had a puzzled expression on his face. "No, that'll be all for now," she said, smiling sweetly. "Thank you."

He shrugged, then walked off.

Sanchez turned her attention back to the three around the table. Alice stole a glance at the detective, then quickly threw her eyes back to studying the fine lines of fake wood grain in the laminated surface of the tabletop.

"Who's going to tell me what the fuck is going on?" asked Sanchez between gritted teeth.

Trudy was the first to look at Sanchez. "I guess I'd better tell you."

Sanchez crossed her arms over her chest, then leaned back and gave the hairdresser her full attention.

"Sharon left the book in her work station at my shop. Bruce knew it was there. We thought we might be able to use it to track down the killer after Deputy Summers came to see Bruce and reported Sharon was missing."

Sanchez's eyes narrowed and her lips pursed. "What made you think she was murdered?"

"The one red shoe," said Trudy simply.

Sanchez smirked. "Yeah." She nodded her head. "I thought that, too. Ever think of becoming a cop?"

Trudy smiled. She was warming to her subject now. "Naw. I just love a good mystery."

Inside, Sanchez flinched but kept her outward appearance light. Amateur detectives. The worst kind. The kind who screwed up an investigation.

These people didn't know what the hell they had gotten themselves into. The killer was still out there somewhere, and if it turned out to be her husband, which Sanchez thought was the most likely scenario, then Trudy here might become the next victim.

"We took the book and went to Newport, where we tracked down someone who knew Sharon when she lived there…"

"What's the name?" Sanchez asked, interrupting, pulling out her notebook from her suit pocket, placing it on the table, and flipping to the next blank page. She also pulled out a blue plastic ballpoint pen.

"I don't remember the name. Pam, I think…" She lied because she didn't know whom to trust anymore. Her eyes flitted between Bruce and Alice, who sat wide-eyed, watching the interaction between Trudy and the cop. Bruce inclined his head slightly to indicate he understood, while Alice just stared at her, obviously too scared to say anything.

Sanchez had her eyes fixated on her notebook, where she wrote down the name Pam. "So where did you find this woman?"

"In a hairstylist's shop on the main drag in Newport. She worked at a shop called Happy Hair."

"Hmmm… the coast highway. Okay, so what did she tell you about the diary?" Before Trudy could respond, Sanchez's cell phone rang.

It had a short bit of music instead of a normal ring. Trudy recognized the song. It was "When The Saints Go Marching In."

"Shit," said Sanchez, reaching for the phone in the case on her belt.

As the suit jacket moved aside, Trudy could clearly see a gun in a holster. She didn't know anything about guns, but it sure looked like it might do some damage.

"Sanchez," said Sanchez, answering the call; her voice was tight and annoyed. "Oh, sorry, sir." Must be her boss, thought Trudy, or maybe her Dad. Don't be too quick to judge, lady.

She thought about Sharon. The woman had deceived her, but it was her no-good boozer of a husband who was sending their marriage into the dumper, not Sharon.

Drinking, and arguing about drinking, seemed to be all they'd been doing since they came to Fairview. Maybe Sharon had done her a favor.

She stole a glance at Bruce. He was a nice guy who'd lost his big sister. She understood his anger and his need to find the killer. But she needed to save herself, and since she'd come this far, she had to see the thing through. To hell with the consequences.

Sanchez didn't say anything after she closed her phone; instead, she held it in one hand with her eyes closed.

"What's wrong?" asked Bruce.

"They found another body," said Sanchez, her eyes still closed and her voice flat.

"A woman. We don't know who it is yet, but someone walking their dog found her near your house."

She opened her eyes and looked squarely at Trudy. "That was Sheriff Miller. A nude female body was found in the bushes by the side of the street. We think she was raped, then strangled. No confirmation until the coroner has a look at her, of course, but the condition of the body seems to suggest the rape, and the red marks on the neck are consistent with strangulation. I don't think I need to go into the other gory details. Strangulation is a rather unpleasant way to die."

"Did she have large breasts?" asked Bruce.

Sanchez gave him a look of disgust.

He almost smiled. "No, it's not what you're thinking. We saw a blonde hairdresser get into a blue pickup truck while we were in Newport. Does she match that description?"

The detective's eyes narrowed. "How the hell do you know what she looks like?"

"We watched a big-breasted blonde leave the hair shop from across the street," said Bruce matter-of-factly. "After we spoke with her."

Sanchez replaced her notebook in her suit jacket and slipped her cell phone back into the holster on her belt. "Yeah, while I can't say for sure, the body fits that general description." She sighed. "I knew this was gonna be a bad day. I should have stayed in bed."

Sanchez shook her head. "You guys may be doing suspicious shit, but one thing's for sure: None of you could have done this. You can't be in more than one place at the same time, can you?" Pausing to lift her coffee cup to her lips, she took a sip of the now cold beverage. "Now, why don't we cut the bullshit you guys have been feeding me and get down to the real reason those women are dead, shall we?"

Trudy smiled to herself. Sanchez was right: they'd better get back to hunting for this killer.

Twenty-Three

MILLER, THE WHITE STYROFOAM COFFEE CUP in his right hand, gazed down at the broken and bruised corpse of Liz. He shook his head. What a waste, he thought. If only she hadn't talked to them, things would be okay right now and she wouldn't have had to die.

The deep purple bruise ringing her throat showed that she'd struggled for life. It impressed him that she fought. She had been such a worthless bitch otherwise. Sex, dope, and partying were all she cared about in that empty head of hers. No, he corrected himself, empty life.

He knelt down, and with the long fingers of his left hand, he closed her eyelids to cover the vacant stare. Good night my sweet, he thought.

"Sheriff." It was Summers, coming up behind him. "Should I set up the crime scene tape around this area so we're ready for the coroner and the CSU guys from Portland?"

Miller glanced over his shoulder at the deputy holding the large roll of shiny yellow police tape that had seen a lot of use lately.

"Yeah. You better mark off the whole area, from the edge of the woods and all along this road to the bottom of the hill. There might be evidence all over this side of the road."

Rising to his full height, his eyes remained on Liz's pale corpse. He recalled the warmth of her soft skin under his touch. Now she was cold and would soon become stiff with rigor.

Finally, Miller turned away and headed for his white cruiser. Once there, he plucked the microphone from the holder on the dash. He thumbed the mike button. "Glenda, this is John."

Glenda, his wife of ten years, was at their home, where she monitored the radio for the Sheriff's Department. She received a small salary, but not as much as a full-time dispatcher would make. It kept the town's policing costs down. The town elders liked that part of the deal they'd made with him when he accepted the job.

"Yeah, John, go ahead," said Glenda's voice over the car radio speaker.

"Put me through to the coroner's office, will you?"

"Not another one? What the hell kinda town have we moved to, John?"

"Just put me through, will you, please," he snapped. He was beginning to lose patience with his wife. Someone he had little time for, as it was.

"Okay, okay, right away. Don't be mad."

There was pause, then a man's voice came over the radio. "Rowland," said Doctor Lawrence Rowland, state coroner, from his office in Eugene.

"Doc, I got another one."

"Son of a bitch, another one? You got an epidemic going on over there or sumthin'?"

"No, Doc, we're just having a little streak of bad luck is all."

The doctor sighed. "Okay, give me the particulars and I'll be there in two an' a half after I have a shower."

Miller spent the next ten minutes describing what he'd seen, the approximate age of the victim, and other details concerning Liz's corpse. He left out her name, instead calling her Jane Doe.

"Got it. See you in a bit."

Replacing the mike in it's holder, Miller stepped out of his car and leaned across the roof to watch Summers stringing tape around the area where Liz's body lay.

He glanced up the street to the house where Rocky Wilson lived. There weren't any lights inside, though he knew the drunken asshole was there. It was an important detail for Sanchez to learn when she arrived. And he knew she'd be here soon. His eyes twinkled as a grin spread across his rugged, tanned face. Sometimes opportunity had a way of falling right into your path.

***

Sanchez had one arm resting across the top of the booth cushion. The fingers of her other hand played with her now empty coffee cup. Her dark eyes were free of expression as she listened to Trudy's explanation of what they'd discovered about Sharon Carstairs' murder. She interrupted twice to ask questions during the lengthy explanation, but for the most part remained silent, listening intently to what the hairdresser had to say.

Bruce jumped in occasionally, adding his opinions to what Trudy was saying. Alice also seemed intent on the conversation, but seemed nervous. Her eyes shifted between Bruce and Trudy and she totally avoided looking at Sanchez.

Finally, when Trudy explained Alice had been lying to them, Sanchez dropped her arm from the back of the booth and leaned forward to gaze into Alice's eyes. Alice avoided the detective's stare by looking down to her half-eaten salad. Trudy caught the slight smile that crossed Sanchez's face; her dark eyes shifted briefly in Trudy's direction, then back at Alice.

Trudy ended her story with the blue truck driving away with one of the blonde Barbie's in the passenger seat, a curly-haired man driving. She told Sanchez the truck's license plate number.

Sanchez grunted, keeping her eyes on Alice. "You know, I think you may be on to something."

Alice's eyes widened and her hands began to tremble. "Listen, you guys, I didn't do anything wrong, so back the fuck off." She was trying to sound confident, but her involuntary trembling said she was anything but confident.

"Let's talk later, Alice," said Sanchez. "Right now, though, I've got a crime scene to get to." Sanchez slid to the edge of the booth's bench seat. "And a license plate number to check."

"You know, you guys can always follow me. After all, Trudy does live down the street from the crime scene, and it's still a free country last time I checked, so why not come along?" She eyed Trudy, who grinned. "It might be interesting for us all."

With that, Sanchez left the table.

She smiled to herself when she heard Trudy say, "So, Bruce, we goin' or not?"

"Yeah, and I'll keep an eye on her," he said. Sanchez stopped and turned to see Bruce grab Alice's arm, and as inconspicuously as possible, start to lead her out of the restaurant. Alice had resigned herself to her fate and made no effort to break the large man's grip, which would have been futile anyway.

"I'll see you all at Trudy's place."

***

Once outside the restaurant, Trudy slipped behind the wheel of her red POS while Alice sat in the back and Bruce sat beside her in the passenger seat as before. She tried to start the car but the electronic pickup had finally given up and the car would not start. They sat in silence, listening to the echo of the raindrops bouncing off the thin metal roof. *What now?* Trudy thought.

Suddenly Trudy froze. Sanchez would think they'd ditched her and were running as if they were guilty. Which we aren't. "Damn this piece of shit," Trudy said, kicking the pedals with her feet. Her hands gripped the steering wheel so hard her knuckles turned white.

"We need to get to your house," said Bruce, his voice calm.

Trudy shifted to look at him. "No fucking kidding. And how do you propose we do that if you're so fucked-up smart?"

"Hitch hike," suggested Alice from the backseat.

Bruce shrugged. "What choice do we have?"

Trudy waved one hand at the rain falling outside. It wasn't that warm in the car, but at least it was dry. Bruce gave her a withering look. Trudy sighed. "All right let's get going. The sooner we get out there, the sooner I'm home."

She and Bruce opened their car doors simultaneously and got out. Immediately, raindrops began to spill down the necks of their jackets.

Trudy winced.

Alice climbed out of the rear seat aided by Bruce, who held the passenger seat forward, and stood next to them.

"Eww," Alice said, her face squished as if she were sucking on a lemon as the heavy raindrops hit her head, face, and neck. "It's cold," she said

"I think she said that for all of us," Bruce said with a sloppy grin on his face. Trudy couldn't resist, she grinned in kind. They headed for the side of the highway and hoped someone would take pity on them and give them a lift—part, if not all, the way.

As they walked, Trudy tapped Bruce on the shoulder and he glanced at her. She silently mouthed the word 'sorry' to which he grinned and shrugged. She smiled and put one arm across his broad shoulders and gave him a quick hug, then they parted and continued to walk side by side.

Twenty-Four

TRUDY WAVED TO MR. JOHNSON IN HIS '83 PONTIAC PARISENNE when she saw him coming toward them. He pulled the large car to the side of the road and reached across the front seat to open the passenger door.

Trudy, Bruce, and Alice had been hitchhiking for twenty minutes and their clothes were soaking wet. Alice was shivering. Trudy had never been so thankful to see anyone. "Thanks, Mr. Johnson, we would really appreciate a ride to my house. My car broke down. Turn off onto Bard, please."

Mr. Johnson explained he was on his way to pick up the newspaper and a carton of milk for his wife's tea, but readily agreed to take them to Trudy's house. The car seats were slick vinyl, so he assured them he would dry them off later and not to worry.

"Nice car," said Bruce, fitting his bulk into the front seat next to Trudy, whose arm brushed against Mr. Johnson. Alice sat in the back seat, gazing out the window at the rain.

Mr. Johnson had the radio turned off so the interior of the car was filled with the sound of the rain and the steady swish of the wipers doing their best to keep up.

"Yup, she's a beauty all right," said Mr. Johnson. "All original parts, too. Did the work myself." His voice evident with pride.

"You a mechanic?" asked Bruce.

Mr. Johnson laughed. "Nope, retired school teacher, but I've been interested in cars since I was a boy. This car was my retirement project. Kept me busy for quite a few years, let me tell you." He nodded his head knowingly.

He turned onto Bard Street and started down the ambling road between large stands of fir trees.

"This is the right way?" asked Johnson.

"Yeah, thanks," said Trudy glumly. She began to shiver as the dampness penetrated her clothes. She hugged herself tightly.

Bruce must have seen her shiver because he placed one arm around her shoulders and pulled her close, adding his body heat to hers. Her sad eyes gazed at his young face and she smiled thinly. He kept his eyes intent on the road ahead.

She knew he cared about her. He really did. Certainly more than that piece of shit husband of hers. Odd how men sometimes came into your life when it was too late. In a different time, she and Bruce could've been soul mates instead of friends. They'd grown close in a short time.

"How's Mrs. Johnson?" asked Trudy, trying to make conversation with Mr. Johnson.

He shrugged. "Okay, I guess. She's been going to Molly's Hair on State since you've been closed. When you gonna be back at work?"

Trudy shrugged. "Don't know, exactly."

Mr. Johnson chuckled. "Well, I hope it's soon. The old broad is really bending my ear about you not being at the shop. She hates having her routine disturbed these days."

Trudy caught the inflection in his voice. Mrs. Johnson's Alzheimer's must be getting worse.

"You tell her she'll be the first person I call when I re-open. Okay, Mr. Johnson?"

"I'd really appreciate it, Trudy," Mr. Johnson said, sounding relieved. "I'll let her know."

The car made one final turn and Trudy's house came into view. It was dark and they could see two police cars, lights flashing, farther down the street. A line of yellow police tape ran down one side of the road.

Two uniformed men stood by one of the police cars. It was the sheriff and his deputy. On the other side of the road was Detective Sanchez's white unmarked car. Mr. Johnson pulled the Pontiac into Trudy's driveway and stopped. He pulled the gearshift lever until the big V8 was idling.

"Well, here we are." He gazed down the street at the police cars. "Wonder what's going on? Too far from the beach to be another floater."

Trudy felt Bruce's body tense against her. She patted his shoulder and he relaxed. Lifting her head, she gazed into his eyes. They were angry and brimming with tears.

When they got out of the car, Trudy thanked Mr. Johnson for the ride. He said good-bye, backed the large car into the street, and quickly disappeared up the rise in the road.

Trudy, followed by Bruce and Alice, walked up the driveway. Trudy retrieved her key from her purse and unlocked the door.

The garage door was closed, but she knew Rocky was home from the odor of stale beer and cigarettes that assaulted her when she entered.

Alice wrinkled her nose and Bruce sighed.

"Let's see what the son of a bitch has been doing while we've been busy saving his ass," said Trudy.

After closing the front door behind them, Trudy flipped on one of the light switches. The swag ceiling lamp lit up the foyer, giving it an eerie, orange glow. They took off their coats and Trudy hung them in the closet.

Climbing the stairs to the living room, they discovered scattered newspapers and empty beer cans strewn over the coffee table, the end tables, and the floor.

Rocky lay face-up on the couch, wearing blue striped boxers, a white undershirt, and black socks. He was snoring loudly. The TV was still on, offering the only light in the room. The front curtains were pulled shut, obviously to keep the world out and the slob from being seen by the world. Not a bad thing, thought Trudy. Picking up the remote, she turned off the television.

Bruce moved to stand over the snoring Rocky Wilson. Bruce pinched his nose and waved the air, his features squished. Rocky's sweaty face was coated with a few days' worth of beard, a patchwork of gray and black stubble covering his puffy face. The smell coming off him was of stale beer, urine, and sweat. Trudy covered her mouth and nose. Her husband was a real mess. Worse than ever before.

Bruce tapped him lightly on the right cheek and then pinched Rocky's cheeks between the fingers of his left hand. "Whew. Does he stink, or what? This guy's been on a major fucking bender," said Bruce, with undisguised disgust in his voice.

"Yeah," said Trudy. Maybe it was over. Maybe she should give up on him.

"How could he have killed that girl down the street when he was like this?" asked Alice.

"He couldn't have," said Bruce slowly. Rocky moaned, then turned on his side to curl into a fetal position.

Trudy agreed. Rocky hadn't killed anyone. She knew none of them had, so who killed Sharon, Emily, and the Barbie? Someone who had a blue pickup matching Rocky's, that's who. Maybe Sanchez had run the license plate by now.

As if a light suddenly came on, Trudy realized where they might have an ally. The doorbell rang, interrupting her thoughts.

She asked Bruce to answer the bell. "Open up, this is the police," a man's voice drifted up the stairs. Trudy followed Bruce to the bottom of the stairs.

Bruce opened the door to discover Deputy Summers, his thumbs hooked off his gun belt. His hazel eyes were stone cold and he wore an arrogant sneer on his lean features.

Trudy really was beginning to hate the man. Behind him stood Detective Sanchez, her dark eyes watchful, her tanned face free of expression. Her suit jacket had been hitched behind her holster, exposing the automatic pistol, the restraining strap unbuttoned. These two meant business.

"Mrs. Wilson," said the deputy, who tipped his cap politely. "We're here to arrest your husband." He spoke matter-of-factly. "May we come in?"

Trudy knew she couldn't refuse, even if she wanted to. If she made it difficult for them, they would simply get a warrant and wait out front until either Rocky came out or the warrant arrived.

Then, if they needed to, they'd force their way in. Any way you sliced it, they were going to take him.

Not a bad idea really, when you think about it, she thought. At least I'd be rid of the guy.

"You got a warrant?" It was Bruce who spoke first.

She glanced up at his dark eyes, which were hard. His expression was serious. She got a slight glint in his eye when he slid her a quick glance. He had something in mind, so she would play along.

"Yeah," she said. "You got a warrant?"

"Now, Mrs. Wilson, we don't want to make this any more difficult than we have to—" began Deputy Summers.

"Let me handle this," said Sanchez, stepping forward to stand beside Summers.

Summers frowned. "I don't think the sheriff'd like that."

Sanchez smiled thinly. "Let me handle the sheriff."

Summers shook his head. "Okay, be my guest. After you."

"May I come in and speak with you and your husband, Mrs. Wilson? I promise I won't arrest your husband. At least until the warrant arrives. That's the best I can do, okay?"

Trudy hesitated, then glanced at Bruce, who nodded. Looking back at Sanchez, she said, "All right. You can come in, but the Deputy has to stay outside."

Summers' mouth hung open and his eyes were wide. "But…"

"Wait here," said Sanchez, entering the house and slamming the door in his face before he could protest. Sanchez turned to look through the peephole. Trudy heard Summers grumble and then his boots thudded on the steps leading to the driveway.

The detective smiled when she turned to look at Bruce and Trudy. "Now let's finish our little talk."

They walked upstairs where Alice sat in the La-Z-Boy, staring out the front picture window.

Rocky was still asleep on the couch, snoring loudly. His chubby frame rose and fell with each breath.

"Whew," said Sanchez. "He's a little ripe, isn't he?"

Trudy nodded. "Yeah. He's my little loveable drunk," she said sarcastically

Sanchez's eyes narrowed. "I understand." She paused to sit in one of the wing chairs across from the couch. "I have to start by asking you something which may be uncomfortable," said Sanchez.

Trudy sat down in a matching chair and crossed her legs.

"Do you think your husband killed that girl down the road or any of the other victims?"

"No," said Trudy firmly. "It isn't possible. My husband may be a drunk, and more recently a skirt chaser, but he's incapable of hurting anyone. I think I know who did, though."

Sanchez's eyebrows arched in surprise. "Really? And who do you think did these crimes?"

"We need to find out who owns a blue pickup truck and lives in Fairview," she glanced at Rocky's sleeping form. "Besides Rocky."

Sanchez nodded. "Yeah, that's what I thought, too. I called my boss and he's added the license plate number of that blue truck to the list of items he's checking out for me."

She reached into her suit pocket to extract her notebook. Trudy glanced at Bruce and rolled her eyes. More twenty questions.

"He did share some interesting tidbits with me about each of you, though," said Sanchez, looking up from the now open notebook, a slight smile on her lips.

"Bruce Carstairs," she read. "Three speeding tickets in the past two years. One drunk and disorderly charge, stayed due to lack of evidence. You work for a known Hells Angel bike shop in Seattle, but appear to have no discernable links to the bikers. Despite your appearance." She smirked.

"Rocky Wilson," she nodded at Rocky, who emitted a loud snore as she continued. "One arrest. Public drunkenness. Here in Fairview. Person of interest in a murder investigation."

Pausing to flip the page, she said, "Trudy Wilson. Nope, nothing on your record. You're clean." She smiled. "Good news."

The smile disappeared when her brown eyes locked on Alice, who paled visibly.

"Alice Morrison, aka Alice Miller. Former prostitute from LA. Sixteen arrests over the past five years, no convictions. Nothing else since a year ago when you changed your name and moved to Fairview."

Bruce and Trudy stared at Alice in shock. She's hiding from something after all, thought Trudy. The sweet little innocent girl act was clearly a disguise for a much darker past.

Alice's eyes turned hard and her expression became one of pure anger and hatred. Her pretty face had lost all its beauty as the true person she was came out. The sweet young thing had fully transformed to the experienced, hard-bitten hooker. She clearly has no heart of gold—more like coal, thought Trudy.

"Damn you pigs, you're all so fuckin' smart. I'm trying to leave that life behind me, but you never want to let us forget, do you?"

"Miller?" Bruce said, a deep frown creasing his forehead. "Any relation to Sheriff Miller?"

"Of course not. He's a fuckin' cop, isn't he? I don't have no pigs in my family," Alice said, her tone defiant and arrogant.

Bruce's frown deepened.

"So what's the connection?" asked Trudy, turning to look at Sanchez.

The detective shrugged. "I have no idea. Niece, maybe, or cousin. I couldn't find any connection whatsoever." Her dark eyes narrowed. "Maybe I better ask the sheriff."

"He won't tell you anything," said Alice, her bare arms crossed over her chest, her eyes cool as blue ice.

"Well, he might think you have talked to us."

Alice's eyes went wide and her already-pale skin drained to a chalky pallor. She began to tremble. "You won't tell him I said anything, will you?" she whispered.

"You better believe I will," said Sanchez firmly.

Trudy thought she could feel Alice's fear fill the room. She wasn't faking it this time. She was deathly afraid.

Alice shook her head. "You bitch. You're lying."

"Try me."

Alice buried her face in her hands. Her body shook as heaving sobs racked her slight frame. "He'll kill me," she sobbed.

Like an angler reeling in the catch of the day, Sanchez leapt on the girl's words. "Who?" she asked, moving forward to rest on the edge of the chair. Her dark eyes bored into Alice.

"Larry." Trudy, Bruce, and the detective exchanged glances.

"Who's Larry?" asked Sanchez, turning her attention back to the girl.

"Larry Biggs. A cop from LA. You guys know about him, right?" her red-rimmed eyes glanced about at the three stunned faces.

"LB," said Bruce, his voice a whisper. "I knew it." He stepped up to the hooker, raised a closed fist, and landed a punch square in the center of her face.

She stumbled backward until she collapsed on top of Rocky.

With one hand, Alice held her nose as blood seeped between her fingers and ran down her cheeks. Trudy could see one eye beginning to swell already. Alice began to cry, then scream like a mad woman.

Rocky woke suddenly and pushed Alice off him. She landed on her butt next to the couch. He sat up, staring at the girl with bloody trails down her face and hands. She was blinking furiously, trying to clear her vision.

"Did you have to do that, Bruce? She is the only living witness we have."

Bruce was breathing heavily and his face was red. His hazel eyes burned with anger. "Yeah. It made me feel better." He pointed at Alice. "She let the son of a bitch kill my sister and she did nothing to stop him."

"You don't know that," said Trudy softly.

Trudy knelt down next to the injured girl. "Now, Alice, we're going to have a long talk, and you're going to tell us everything, aren't you?"

Alice nodded.

"Okay, kids, that's enough time in the sandbox," interrupted Sanchez. "I think little Alice here is primed and ready to tell us all she knows." Alice glared daggers at the detective.

"What the fuck is going on?" asked Rocky, clearly upset that his sleep had been disturbed.

"Rocky, why don't you shut the fuck up and go back to sleep," said Trudy angrily.

He shrugged his shoulders, lay down again, and curled up to face the back of the couch. Trudy shook her head and shared a look of disgust with Bruce.

Trudy helped Alice to her feet, then led her into the kitchen. Sanchez and Bruce followed. Trudy sat Alice at the kitchen table while she went to the freezer above the fridge to get some ice to reduce the swelling. Bruce and Sanchez sat down, as well. Bruce glared at the girl, who had the look of the defeated.

Alice knew her time to come clean had arrived.

Twenty-Five

When Summers strode up to Sheriff Miller, he could see right away that the sheriff wasn't happy to see him returning alone without Rocky and Trudy Wilson and Detective Sanchez. Summers' stomach muscles tightened.

"Where's Sanchez?" asked Miller, his voice cold, his blue eyes glaring at Summers as if he were a bug about to be stepped on. "And my two prisoners?"

"That biker seemed to know the law pretty good," said Summers. "He wanted to see a warrant and since we didn't have one…"

"Cut the bullshit and tell me where Detective Sanchez is, right now."

He said it with such force a slight tremor ran through Summers body. The sheriff was a tough boss, but he'd never spoken to him with this much intensity.

He pointed at the Wilson's house. "In there with them."

Miller sighed heavily. "Never send a coward when you can send a lion," he said in a low murmur. "You wait here in the car for the coroner to arrive; I'll go speak to them."

Summers nodded, grim, but thankful he'd gotten off so easily. He sensed he was lucky Miller hadn't fired him on the spot.

Miller walked down the road until he was at the front door. He pounded on it until his fist was as red as his mood and pressed the doorbell five times, but there was no sign of activity inside. He tried the doorknob but the door was locked.

He marched back to Summers' cruiser, leaned through the window, and glared into Summers eyes. "It looks like our suspects have taken the detective hostage. I want you to drive back to the office and call the state police office. Tell them to send an ERT."

"Sheriff, why don't we just use the radio? Like you did to get hold of the coroner?"

Miller smiled slyly. "Summers, who's the sheriff, you or me?"

"Yes, sir," said Summers, his eyes darting toward the house. Summers started the engine of the cruiser. "I'm on my way."

Miller stood back and watched Summers disappear up the hill. He walked to his cruiser, pulled out his car keys, and opened the trunk.

The trunk lid swung upward revealing a padlocked gun case affixed to the trunk bed. He opened the padlock with a key on the same ring and flipped the lid open.

Inside was an M16 assault rifle with two clips of ammunition. He would take care of the witnesses himself. He'd already concluded that Alice had talked. Now they all had to die.

By the time Summers returned, they would be dead and he would be the hero who had brought a dangerous gang of criminals to swift justice.

After ensuring the rifle was loaded, he leaned it against the bumper of the car, pocketed two additional ammo clips, and reached for his body armor.

He slipped the vest over his head using the Velcro strips to secure it tightly about his upper body. He didn't normally wear the vest because it was too restricting, but Sanchez had a pretty mean automatic in her holster. She was no doubt quite accurate with the gun, so he decided the additional insurance of the body armor was warranted.

Flipping the safety off on the side of the rifle, he cocked the weapon. He started back toward the dark house with a confident swagger. He was ready to kill.

Miller walked up the street toward the house. The weight of the smooth, cool rifle in his hands was minimal given the strength of his sinewy arms beneath his uniform shirt. He smelled the salt in the air and felt invigorated. He would dump the bodies in the ocean afterward. All the evidence of their existence would be washed out to sea. So many tragedies. He smiled to himself.

His cold blue eyes were trained on the front door of the split-level house, scanning for possible threats. He knew he had them out-gunned, but it paid to be cautious. Working the streets of LA had been an invaluable school for inflicting violence on others.

Climbing the steps to the front door, he shifted to one side to avoid any direct fire from inside through the thin wood.

He gripped the rifle in one hand and rapped on the door with his knuckles. He waited. No answer. His heart beat hard against his ribs. He loved the excitement of the hunt. The hunt was as much fun as the kill.

Enough of this shit. Leveling the rifle at the doorknob, he depressed the trigger. A three-shot burst shattered the wood surrounding the knob. He took a step back, then with one swift kick, crashed the door inward with a bang. If they hadn't known he was coming, they most certainly knew now he'd arrived.

Silence. No sounds of movement. *Odd.* They should have screamed or something.

He stepped inside, crouching slightly, keeping the rifle butt pressed into his shoulder as he swept the stairs, sighting down the gun barrel. No threats, yet.

Moving slowly up the carpeted stairs, he kept the rifle trained at the top of the staircase. Silence.

Once at the top, he saw that the living room was empty except for a worn couch and a couple of chairs. On the coffee table was an ashtray, overflowing with gray ash and cigarette butts. Empty beer cans and old newspapers were strewn about the room.

He moved to the kitchen off the living room and saw that it, too, was deserted.

He lowered the rifle. The coffeepot was still on; it was half full. The coffee smelled over-cooked. They must be hiding in one of the bedrooms. That won't save them, he thought. Smirking to himself, he left the kitchen.

The hallway leading to the bedrooms was dark. He quickly found the switch that turned on the hall light. He moved up the hall, sweeping the rifle back and forth. He kept his finger pressed against the trigger, ready should Sanchez appear.

The first door he came to was stuck partly open. He burst through and found the room empty except for a single bed with a bright orange coverlet thrown over it. There was a small closet, but the slatted doors were standing open.

He grunted and went back into the hallway. The next door was closed. Now we're getting somewhere, he thought. I'm gonna enjoy this.

Miller stood with his back to the wall beside the bedroom door. He tried the doorknob.

It was locked, but the door itself was a typical, hollow, interior door, so he could break the lock easily.

Moving to stand in front of the door, he took a step back and, after raising one booted foot, kicked the door to splinters. It violently slammed into the wall with a loud crack. Bursting in, he sprayed the room with bullets. The rain of 5.56 mm bullets shredded the furniture inside. After the thirty-shot magazine was empty, all that remained was the odors of burnt gunpowder. What were missing were the bloody, bullet-ridden bodies. Smoke from the barrel drifted lazily in the still air.

Fuck. Where were they? Ejecting the spent magazine, he slapped in a new one. His heart raced and after removing his earplug from his right ear he strained to hear any sounds of his prey. He froze, listening intently. In the distance, he heard a car motor start.

Damn. He'd left his keys in the trunk lock. He knew immediately what was happening. The bastards were stealing his car. They must've gone out the back and gone around when he burst in the front door. *Fuck.*

Running from the room, he raced down the hall, took the stairs two at a time, and ran out the front door. He caught a glimpse of his cruiser, cresting the hill. Raising the M16 to his shoulder, he sighted down the barrel just as the car disappeared. Lowering the gun, he smashed the door with his left fist. Bitches. They and their biker boy-toy had to die.

He had been going to give them quick, easy deaths, but not now. Now he was determined to ensure they suffered before they died. But he had to move fast.

***

Trudy, Bruce, and Sanchez sat in rapt attention while Alice explained how she had met Biggs in Los Angles five years ago. He was the vice cop who had arrested her so many times she'd lost count. He took money from the girls, and had frequently accepted payoffs for protection from drug dealers.

She had left LA two years ago and moved to Fairview to get away from the dangers of street life. She had been enjoying her newfound freedom until she met Sharon's new boyfriend, Sheriff Miller. Miller was Larry Biggs.

When she confronted him about his criminal past, hoping to blackmail him, he threatened to kill her if she told anyone the truth about him. Turning the tables on her, he instead extorted sex from her in return for not revealing her true origins to her roommates or the other people in Fairview. He reminded her that small-town people didn't take too kindly to ex-prostitutes.

Miller was dating Sharon and everything seemed fine until he started to physically abuse her. Alice finally told Sharon and Emily who Miller really was, hoping they'd stay away from him.

Unfortunately, Sharon had tried to use the information to blackmail Miller. It was then events started to spiral out of control. After Sharon and Emily were killed, Alice thought she'd hide out with Bruce and Trudy, hoping she'd be safe. Then, as soon as she could, she'd slip away and start a new life somewhere else.

At the end of her story, she began to sob. Trudy ran one hand through Alice's blonde hair. Though Alice had lied to them, Trudy's heart still ached for the young woman.

She'd obviously been through hard times Trudy could only imagine. "It's okay, dear. We won't let Biggs hurt you."

The sound of a car engine made Sanchez look out the window. Her brow wrinkled.

"What is it?" asked Trudy.

"Strange. Summers is leaving." Sanchez nodded. "Miller's up to something."

Sanchez pulled her cell phone off her belt and flipped it open. "Damn it. The battery's dead. I need to use your phone."

Instead of answering, Trudy stepped forward. Together, they watched Miller open the trunk of his car.

Miller took out a rifle and pulled on body armor over his uniform shirt. He walked to the house. There was a pounding at the front door and the doorbell rang repeatedly.

Sanchez pulled her pistol and continued to watch through the window. "Summers is gone," she whispered. "It's the sheriff."

Sanchez glanced at Trudy, then eyed her pistol.

Trudy's eyes went wide as she discerned the detective's meaning. Sanchez's gun wasn't going to stop someone armed with serious firepower wearing body armor.

"Do you own a gun?" Sanchez asked.

"Are you kidding?"

The detective's jaw line hardened. "Well, we're about to have a big problem. Miller, or whatever his name is, is headed this way armed for bear, and unless we have some way to stop him, we're all dead meat." She released the curtain. It sighed as it dropped back into place, covering the window.

Trudy rushed into the kitchen and picked up the receiver from the yellow rotary telephone hanging on the wall.

She listened for a few seconds, then replaced it. "It's dead. Miller must have cut the line."

Twenty-Six

Sanchez insisted on driving. Her tanned fingers grasped the steering wheel tightly, turning her knuckles white. Her dark eyes flirted with the rearview mirror as she gunned the white police cruiser away from the side of the road. Trudy, seated in the passenger seat, swiveled her head as they sped past the house, willing the front door to remain closed.

Bruce sat in the back seat, behind Trudy. Rocky, replete in his underwear, sat behind Sanchez, his head leaning against the car's doorframe. Alice was in the middle of the back seat.

"Do you see him?" asked Sanchez, her dark eyes fixed on the top of the hill.

"Not yet," said Trudy. "Wait. Yes. I see him; he's still got his rifle. He looks very pissed off."

"Fuck 'em," said Sanchez.

"Amen," growled Bruce.

"Where we goin'?" asked Trudy.

Sanchez's lips formed a grin. "We have to get rid of this car and get some other transportation. Then we have to get outta Dodge."

"I know just where to go," said Trudy.

Sanchez took her eyes off the road momentarily and looked quizzically at the hairdresser.

"Head for the sheriff's station. I have a plan," said Trudy.

Sanchez shrugged. What did she have to lose at this stage? Trudy was right. The woman had remarkable insight for a civilian. The cruiser would be a like beacon for Miller, so they had to do something with it fast before he murdered them all.

***

A light rain began to fall just as Sanchez stopped the car in front of the sheriff's office and turned off the engine.

Trudy's plan was simple: Sanchez would go in to the office and tell Summers she had escaped from the house. Then she would disarm him and lock him in one of the jail cells. She'd find the keys for Rocky's truck, which had been parked at the station since the night it was impounded. They would park Miller's cruiser at the rear of the building, so he wouldn't see it immediately when he returned.

Hopefully, Summers was as dumb as he looked and fell for her ruse.

Sanchez got out of the car and quickly disappeared through the front door. After a few minutes when she didn't reappear, Bruce got out and went to the door. With the flat of one hand, he slowly pushed the door open.

He smiled back at Trudy, then stepped inside, closing the door behind him.

Trudy trembled when a gunshot shattered the silence. She and Alice scrambled out of the car.

211

Then before Trudy could stop her, Alice ran across the main road, playing chicken with the cars and trucks. Some honked their horns as they swerved to miss her. Fortunately, for her, none hit her and she disappeared inside a café across the street.

Trudy moved to the front door of the sheriff's office and was about to reach for the doorknob when suddenly it burst open. She stumbled backward as Bruce, followed closely by Sanchez, walked out.

"Did we scare you?" asked Bruce, a sardonic grin on his face.

"You fucking asshole," she said. "You guys scared the shit out of me."

"Summers objected to us taking these." Sanchez dangled the car keys for Rocky's truck in the air in front of Trudy, a smile across her face. "The big guy here clobbered him from behind before he shot me. The bullet has been added the to the sheriff's precious collection of pictures on his office wall as a permanent decoration." She frowned. "Do you think there's some symbolism in the fact that the bullet went right through the middle of his forehead in one of the pictures?"

Trudy chuckled. "You guys." She walked back toward the cruiser. "I'll move the car to the back while you two get the truck.

"Where's Alice?" asked Bruce, looking for her.

"She's in the café across the street." Trudy pointed across the road.

"Fuck her," said Bruce. "She's on her own."

"Miller will kill her," said Sanchez. "We gotta do something."

"Right now, we're the only one's who can put an end to these murders. And that must be our first priority, don't you think, Detective?" asked Bruce grimly.

"Alice has been on a destructive path for so long I don't think she knows how to get her life back on track anymore."

Sanchez nodded. "Yeah, I guess you're right." She gazed at the small café wistfully. "I hope she gets out of the café and knows enough to stay out of Miller's cross hairs."

Bruce and Sanchez jogged to the corner of the building while Trudy climbed back into the cruiser. Rocky was still asleep in the backseat, snoring. Sometimes I envy your ability to leave the world even for a short time, she thought. I wish it were that easy for me.

She drove around the building and pulled up next to Rocky's blue pickup, tuned off the engine, and stepped out. Bruce already sat behind the steering wheel of the truck, waiting for her, with Sanchez next to him. She indicated Rocky, asleep in the rear seat.

Bruce grimaced, stepped out, and walked over to the cruiser. He opened the rear door and lifted Rocky out, then carried him fireman-style to the flat bed of the truck. There was a canvas cover over the truck's bed. While it was wet on the top, it was also waterproof, so the bed itself was dry.

Bruce pulled back the canvas tarp, then laid Rocky spread-eagled on the cool metal. Bruce threw the canvas cover over Rocky's still-sleeping form. Trudy shook her head and grimaced; her husband really could sleep through anything.

"You know, I'd like to leave the son of a bitch for that crazy sheriff," said Bruce.

Trudy patted his shoulder. "I know. Let's go."

Sanchez slid to the middle of the truck's bench seat. Trudy climbed in beside her and Bruce slid behind the wheel again. When he started the engine, the V8 roared to life. Trudy noticed there was half a tank of gas left, so they would need precious time to fill it.

"I'm going to get my bike," Bruce said matter-of-factly.

Sanchez looked at him aghast. "Are you nuts? We have to leave town as soon as possible. It isn't gonna take that murderous son of a bitch long to find us."

Bruce glared at her. "I'm not leaving my bike."

Sanchez looked to Trudy for support. "We have to get the hell outta here."

Trudy shrugged. "If Bruce says we need to get his bike, then we need to get his bike. Besides, it'll mean Rocky won't have to ride in the truck bed the whole way to Portland."

Sanchez shook her head. "I hope you two know what you're doin'."

Bruce backed away from the building. Once sufficiently clear, he shifted into gear and drove out of the parking lot. On the highway, they headed south toward the Overlook Motel. Trudy knew Sanchez was right, but thankfully there was no sign of Miller yet.

Soon they were pulling into the motel parking lot next to Bruce's motorcycle. He'd left it here while they went to Newport. Bruce had had the foresight to put a heavy black plastic cover over the bike to shield it from the rain. It was raining and seemed to be coming harder now. Leaving the engine of the truck running, he stepped out onto the wet pavement.

"I'll start her up, then I'll move Rocky to the front seat."

Trudy nodded.

Bruce pulled the black cover off. His jaw dropped and his cheeks lost their color. "What the fuck!"

A trail of bullet holes ran down the length of the bike, the front and rear tires were flat, and the gas tank had been punctured. His wide face turned red and his hands curled into fists. "I'll kill the son of a bitch who did this to my bike!"

John Miller emerged from the shadows at the side of the building. His rifle was leveled at them. His blue eyes were narrow and his lips formed a twisted grin. Trudy's heart skipped a beat as her breath caught in her throat. They were dead.

"I knew a biker would never leave his precious hog behind." He laughed, sending a chill down Trudy's spine. Mad with power, the bastard had snapped.

Shaking off her fear, Trudy stepped out of the truck, anger boiling from deep within her.

"There's no way you can get away with this," she said slowly. "We know who you really are, Larry."

His blue eyes changed and the smile on his face faded. He stepped clear of the shadows, the gun leveled at Trudy's stomach.

"How do you know that name?"

She'd unnerved him. His confidence was waning.

"You," he said, waving the gun barrel at Sanchez, who was still in the truck's cab. "Get out."

Sanchez slid across the seat, got out, and stood next to Trudy. Trudy caught a glimpse of her gun, still in the holster beneath her suit jacket.

Unfortunately, so did Miller. "Throw your gun over here." He waved the barrel of the rifle to indicate she was to toss her service automatic to the ground in front of him. He blinked away the rainwater running down his forehead into his eyes.

Slowly, Sanchez pulled out her pistol. Trudy watched in horror as she saw Sanchez flip off the pistol's safety. She must think their only hope was to shoot back.

She's gonna get us killed.

Like a slow motion scene in a movie, Trudy watched Sanchez draw her gun.

As she raised it, Miller fired a quick, three-round burst, the bullets shattering Sanchez's legs. She screamed, then collapsed to the ground. Her gun dropped and clattered across the pavement, the sound echoing off the wall of the motel.

Sanchez lay on the wet pavement, her hands grasping at her wounded legs, writhing and moaning in pain. Blood seeped between her fingers, staining the pavement red.

"You shouldn't have done that," said Miller, chuckling a maniacal grin on his face. "I'll finish you later. I want to enjoy watching you suffer for a bit longer before you die."

Miller waved the rifle at the bike. "Step away," he said to Bruce, who glared at him.

Bruce moved to stand beside Trudy. Miller pumped three more shots into the bike's gas tank and gas began to spurt from the bullet holes running down the sides of the gas tank.

"Son of a bitch," breathed Bruce. "Did you really have to do that?" he yelled at Miller, who grinned his eyes wild.

He's lost it, thought Trudy.

"Why not?" Miller asked, laughing like some loony bin escapee. He motioned toward the ocean with his rifle. "Let's go for a little walk. I feel like some fresh air."

Trudy and Bruce turned to walk to the stairs leading to the beach at the bottom of the cliff. The rain was harder now and the wind had picked up, blowing salt air into their faces.

Trudy led the way and Bruce followed close behind, with Miller goading them on, the gun as the incentive. We aren't dead yet, thought Trudy. She knew what Miller had in mind now that his frontal assault plan had been foiled. He'd shoot them, then let the ocean claim the bodies, much like he had done with Sharon.

"Come on," Miller said, prodding Bruce with the barrel of his rifle after moving up close behind him.

"Take it easy with that fuckin' thing, will you," said Bruce menacingly.

"I'll do the talkin', scumbag," said Miller.

After what seemed an eternity, they finally arrived on the beach. Trudy judged that the black volcanic rocks sticking from the gray sand were a least a couple of hundred yards away. Running on the wet sand would slow them down. Her shoulders slumped. They had zero chance of escape now. This was the end.

She had her regrets. Marrying Rocky had been a mistake. Moving here and buying the shop had been a mistake. Trying to solve Sharon's murder, on the other hand, had been the one thing that had made her feel useful for the first time in a long time.

While the results were not going to turn out the way she'd hoped, it had been a welcome distraction from her mounting problems.

She glanced at Bruce out of the corner of one eye. Meeting him had been the best thing that had happened to her in years. They could've been good friends; he seemed to like her. Not romantically, but as a friend. They'd been through a lot of living these past few days, but now they would be joined in death.

"If you think I'm gonna walk into one of those waves like you made my sister do, you've got another fuckin' think coming," said Bruce.

"You've got a choice, big guy," said Miller, with grim humor in his voice. "I shoot you, then drag you to the edge of the water, where a wave will soon carry you off, or you walk into the surf and take your chances. Some people have survived sneaker waves. Not many, but some." He chuckled. "I understand the undertow is something fierce."

Trudy knew of no one who'd been swept up by a sneaker and lived to tell the tale.

The sound of the crashing waves filled her ears as they moved down the beach toward the surf. Trudy deliberately moved closer to the protruding rocks; she approached them at an angle, hoping Miller wouldn't notice in his arrogant confidence.

Bruce suddenly snarled, then spun to face their kidnapper, his face a mask of rage. The rifle spat twice and Bruce dropped heavily to the sand, face down. He hadn't made a sound when he'd been hit. He lay unmoving on the now red-stained sand.

Trudy stared in horror at her young friend. Why had he done that? Why had he tried to confront this madman—this killer?

"Too bad about your friend," said Miller, shaking his head in mock concern.

Warm tears mingled with the rain to run down her face. She blinked them away; the beach was now a blur. Panic rose in her and her stomach churned. She was really going to die. Miller was really going to murder her. This can't be, Trudy thought. It doesn't make any sense. I'm a hairdresser, I cut hair.

"Listen, Sheriff, I won't tell anyone. I promise. I just want to go back to my normal life, that's all."

He shook his head, a twisted grin on his tanned face. His cold blue eyes fixed on hers. "I don't give a shit if you keep my secret. You and your friends need to die. You must die. Now get going." He motioned for her to keep walking toward the crashing surf.

Her back to him, she closed her eyes and willed her feet to move. The twisting, boiling water became louder with each step. Her knees trembled. Her protectors were gone. This was it, the end of her life. She thought of Rocky. How would he get through life without her to watch over him?

Rocky was an only child and his parents were dead. Her business would certainly fail. She'd miss her clients and her friends.

Tears streamed down her cheeks to be carried away by the strong wind and rain striking her face.

"Faster. Come on, bitch," said the voice behind her.

There was a sudden sharp poke against the small of her back. She winced. It hurt like hell. Anger rose from deep in her stomach, replacing her fear.

Who did this bastard think he was, pushing her around? He was a murderer, a cold-blooded killer. A cold determination came over her. Her eyes became slits as raindrops struck her face. She swiped at her cheeks with her hands. No more tears. The son of a bitch wasn't going to kill Trudy Wilson this easy. Bruce had been right to challenge this psycho.

She spun around to confront him just as there was a sharp crack of a gunshot. She recalled hearing the same sound when she was a girl—when her father took her deer hunting in British Columbia. She could still smell the trees, grasses, and fragrant flowers. And smell the blood.

Miller's eyes were wide as the rifle dropped from his hands, landing on the sand. He slowly dropped to his knees, his blue eyes glazing over, his mouth fixed in an O registering his surprise. Finally he fell forward onto his face and lay still.

Trudy saw that the back of his head was a bloody, oozing mess. Feeling queasy, she gazed at his smashed skull. She ran her hands down the length of her body but didn't feel any pain anywhere she touched.

Her knees turned to jelly and she dropped beside the sheriff's body. Her heart beat rapidly, her entire body still trembling as a sense of relief overwhelmed her.

She wanted to laugh but couldn't manage to make a sound.

Through watery eyes, she saw a figure, dressed in a white undershirt and blue striped boxers, still wearing his black socks and no shoes, coming toward her grasping a handgun in one hand. Good shot, Rocky. My hero.

Emotionally overwhelmed by what had just happened her eyes rolled up in her head and she collapsed onto the wet sand.

***

Trudy's eyes fluttered. Large raindrops were falling on her face. Rocky knelt in the sand next to her, cradling her head in his left arm, stroking her forehead with his right hand.

"It's okay, Trud. I'm here," he said tenderly. There was gentleness in his tone that she hadn't heard in years. It sounded nice.

She gazed up into his moist, red-rimmed eyes and saw great sadness. Reaching up, she wrapped her arms around his neck. "Oh—Rocky." Deep sobs racked her body.

"I know," he said soothingly. "It's over."

She let go and stared at him. "What about Bruce and Detective Sanchez?"

He shook his head. "Now don't you worry about them. I need to get you home. The most important thing right now is your safety."

She sat up and freed herself of her husband's grasp. "No," she said firmly. "First I need to know where Bruce and Sanchez are—right now."

"Okay. Come on." After helping her stand, he supported her with an arm wrapped around her waist. He walked slowly, assisting her in walking across the beach toward the stairs.

As Trudy passed the still form of Sheriff Miller, she realized how close she'd come to death. Anger surged in her. Son of a bitch was gonna shoot me.

Trudy hoped the ocean would swallow up the bastard and take him away forever. Justice had been served and he'd paid the ultimate price for his misdeeds. He was an evil man.

At least Sharon and Emily could rest easy in the knowledge that their killer had been sent to his reward, or his doom, depending on how you viewed such things.

She smirked. Maybe the devil would torment him in hell for eternity. It was a nice thought.

"What is it, Trud?" asked Rocky, his forehead wrinkled.

"Nothing," said Trudy, shaking her head.

They stopped as they came upon Bruce. She stared at him. He'd been a good man. Tears ran in muddy trails down her cheeks, disappearing when they mingled with the rainwater.

A low moan coming from the body of her friend made her stiffen. Her heart beat faster. Freeing herself from Rocky's grasp, Trudy dropped to her knees in the wet sand. She tried to push Bruce over onto his back, but he was too heavy. "Help me," she demanded, casting a pleading look at Rocky.

He shrugged and dropped to his knees beside her.

Together, they pushed Bruce over onto his back, his head lolling. Another moan, only louder this time, not muffled by the sand, escaped from his lips. Having watched enough doctor shows on TV, Trudy grabbed his right wrist and felt for a pulse. It has to be there somewhere, she thought. Frantically, she moved her fingers around his wrist until she could feel a slight, rhythmic bumping under her fingertips.

She looked at Rocky, excitement registering on her face. "He's alive!' She had to stop herself from bursting into tears of joy. "Get help. I'll I stay with him," she said.

"I don't know…" he started to say until he locked eyes with his wife. Without uttering another word, Rocky stood and started running as fast as his large body could carry him toward the stairs to the motel.

Trudy turned her attention back to Bruce and gently patted his pale cheek. "I thought you were dead," she said in a low whisper.

He moaned loudly and his head rolled back and forth.

She scanned his large frame and found two bloody wounds. One in the right shoulder, the other in the right leg. Pulling off her shirt, she tore it down the middle to make a tourniquet for his leg. The other half she'd press into the bullet wound in his shoulder, hoping to stem the flow of blood. She was determined to control the bleeding until help arrived.

Once she had the wounds somewhat under control, she sat down heavily in the sand and gazed at the black ocean. "Don't worry, Sharon," she said, "I'll make sure he doesn't die."

Sanchez would live, too. No one would die on her watch if she could help it.

Twenty-Seven

Two pillows in the hospital bed propped up Bruce when Trudy entered his room carrying a pot of purple pansies. He smiled. His ruddy complexion had returned after having been saved from the brink of death only a day before.

"I see you're alone," he said.

Trudy smiled thinly, her smooth, pale cheeks flushed with a faint, reddish tinge. Without responding, she placed the pot of flowers on the nightstand next to his bed.

After sitting in the chair beside him, Trudy looked around the room, studying it. "Nice digs. Love what you've done with the place."

Bruce chuckled. "Yeah. Kinda nice for the state cops to spring for a private room, don't you think?"

She smirked. "Yeah." Her pale eyes suddenly misted over. "I don't know what to do." She looked away. A single tear ran down her cheek.

"About what?" A frown creased his brow.

She had pushed her mixed feelings about Rocky to the back of her mind the entire time they'd been trying to find the killer. Then he'd come in at the last moment to save her life, and Bruce's. The question now was what to do about her marriage and her business. Both had been teetering on the brink when this all began, and nothing had happened to change that until Rocky shot Miller. Now she had to decide.

Former Deputy Summers had spilled the beans and confessed everything he knew about Miller. Conspiracy and corruption charges were being contemplated by the State Attorney's office, but he hadn't been arrested yet.

Miller had killed Sharon because she was blackmailing him and she was getting more demanding as time went by. Bruce's sister had become so used to using men to get what she wanted that she must've decided blackmailing Miller over his former life as a disgraced LA cop was worth her life. Her mistake. And Emily's, for telling Sharon about Miller. They both paid with their lives.

Miller had chased Sharon down the beach, threatening her with a gun. He must've known tidal conditions would be right for sneaker waves. You had to admire the ingeniousness of the plan. He'd left town immediately after the murder so he'd be out of town when she was reported missing.

Miller hoped the ocean would wipe away any evidence linking him to Sharon's murder. But when one red shoe turned up, the state police, Sanchez in particular, started thinking her death wasn't an accident. The perfect crime had not been so perfect after all.

He must've decided then that anyone who knew the truth about his part in Sharon's death had to die. Miller would have probably killed Summers and his wife to protect himself.

What bothered Bruce was why he'd used a knife to kill poor Emily when he'd used a gun in every other situation. Puzzling. Summers hadn't been able to explain it, either.

"What about Rocky?" asked Bruce.

She nodded her head. "He is my husband, and he did save my life, but does that mean I have to stay married to him…"

"You did take the vow," he said, his voice gentle. It was a pretty lame reason given what had happened, but being married to someone did bring a certain responsibility with it. As the old saying goes, it takes two to make bread, or something like that.

She nodded. "Yeah. That's what makes this so damned difficult."

They sat in silence. Bruce didn't know what else to say.

"So how're you feelin'?" asked Trudy, gazing at him with red-rimmed eyes.

He shrugged. "Not bad. They tell me I'll be outta here in a few days."

"Good."

"How's Sanchez?" asked Bruce.

"She's gonna be okay. She needs a lot of physical therapy, though. Her legs."

Sanchez had already been under the knife twice in the past few days as the surgeons tried to save her legs. They finally succeeded, but Sanchez would need a lot of help before she would be fully mobile again.

Miller's bullets had gone through the bones on both her legs, shattering them. Metal pins had been implanted to keep the bones together. She'd been heavily sedated since the last operation, so Trudy had been unable to speak with her about their shared experience.

It had been Sanchez's gun Rocky used to shoot Miller on the beach. Even he'd been surprised when he'd hit Miller. He wasn't a gun guy and barely knew where the trigger was, never mind how to aim. His shooting the sheriff in the head had truly been one shot in a million. Good for her, lucky for him. If Miller hadn't been taken out, they would all be wearing their wings right now.

"Listen. I gotta go," said Trudy. "I'll come back later with a burger if you want? You must be getting tired of hospital food by now."

"Fuckin' right. Can I have a chocolate milk shake, too?" Bruce asked, with a sloppy grin on his lips.

She stood, nodded, and smiled at him, then placed one hand on his exposed arm. "I'm really sorry about all this," she said in a whisper. Then walked out the door, disappearing into the corridor. His eyes misted over as he watched her go.

The duty nurse came in immediately after Trudy left, forcing Bruce to wipe his eyes clear with the sleeve of his white hospital gown.

"Something wrong?" asked the nurse upon seeing him wiping his eyes.

"Naw, nuthin'" he said, clearing his throat.

***

Once in the parking lot, Trudy stopped to stand beside her red POS. The mechanic had replaced the electronic pickup sensor, so it now ran smoothly. In fact, the car ran smoother than it had since she bought it used five years ago. She drew in a deep breath.

Maybe I'll stop calling it my piece of shit.

She retrieved her car keys from her purse and unlocked the car door, then eased into the driver's seat. She chuckled. Maybe I'll call it my good ol' gal, like its owner.

As she drove out of the parking lot, she glanced at the thin, faux gold watch on her left wrist. She had twenty minutes to get to the bank for the oft-delayed meeting about the business.

Turning right, she drove north on the coast highway. Rolling the driver's side window down, she rested an elbow on the doorframe, using her other hand to steer. The warm breeze was welcoming. She smiled. Today was a good day.

As she drove, she began to hum. A simple tune from her childhood. She occasionally glanced at the cars passing on the other side of the highway.

"Oh, shit!" A familiar face nearly made her drive off the road. Struggling with the wheel, she managed to pull the little car over to the side of the highway, where it lurched to a stop. A car following behind her blew its horn as the driver swerved to miss her. She saw the driver's angry features as he shot by her. He flipped her a one-fingered salute, then was gone.

Her body still shivered from what she'd seen. A blue pickup. Two women inside, one blonde, the other brunette. The blonde driving. The blonde was Alice. She needed to catch her breath. Her chest felt heavy and her heart beat hard.

Alice had disappeared into that café. So far, the state police had been unable to locate her. It was as if she'd disappeared from the face of the earth. Now here she was.

Trudy's mind whirled with uncertainty. What should she do? Call the cops and hope they find her on the highway? Unlikely they would get here before she was gone again. Where was she headed?

Trudy took a deep breath, then gradually took her foot off the brake. Her leg, pressing the pedal, trembled. Checking in the rearview mirror, she saw the highway was clear so she made a u-turn and headed south.

She breathed a sigh of relief. This was going to be easy. She would follow Alice, see where she was headed, then call the cops to arrest her. Too bad she didn't have a cell phone. She'd never seen the need to have one before. Now she wanted to kick herself for not having one.

Peering at the highway ahead, she stepped on the gas pedal in order to gain more speed. Alice would be far ahead already. She needed to catch up. Then she realized that traffic ahead had stopped because someone was making a left against the traffic flow, a gray Cadillac. In the middle of the row of cars and trucks was the blue pickup. Perfect. Her body shook.

She stopped behind the last car in the line, her hands worrying the steering wheel. The gray caddy made the left turn and the traffic began to move again.

Trudy kept her eyes locked on the blue pickup. It drove a few blocks, then turned off to the right down a side street. She did the same. She knew immediately where they were headed. They were headed to the house Alice had shared with Emily and Sharon.

Of course, it made perfect sense. She needed her stuff. The state police had already searched the place and left.

Trudy kept her distance now that she was certain where they were headed. She should report to the cops, but she couldn't help but be curious who Alice was with.

Stopping up the street from the house, Trudy saw the pickup parked in the driveway with no one inside. They must have gone into the house already.

Trudy got out of her car and walked quickly to one of the houses across the street from Alice's. She knocked on the door.

A middle-aged woman with mousy brown hair answered. "Yes, can I help you?" she asked in a pleasant tone.

"Hello. My name's Trudy Wilson. Do you know that house across the street?"

The woman sighed and her smile changed to sadness. "Yes. Unfortunately. A girl died there. Awful." She shook her head sadly.

"Well, someone who was involved is back in that house, and the cops are looking for her."

The woman looked shocked. "Oh, my…"

"Would you please call the cops? Right away?"

The woman nodded. "Do you want to come in?"

"No, I'm gonna go over there and see what they're up to. Just call the cops, okay? State Police. My name is Trudy Wilson, and I'll wait there for them."

The woman nodded and closed the door. Her face had been pale and her lips trembled. She looked as frightened as Trudy felt.

Trudy made her way back to her car and stood beside it for a moment, studying the little bungalow. Why would Alice risk coming back here? Why wouldn't she be long gone?

Over the sound of the breeze that had sprung up suddenly, she thought she heard a muffled cry coming from the house. The sound was so low and so short that Trudy wasn't certain if she'd heard anything at all. Cautiously, she crossed the street and walked around the back of the property.

Moving around to the side Trudy kept her head below the level of the windows, she strained to hear any sign she'd been detected. The stillness of the air made her nervous. The palms of her hands became damp, and beads of sweat formed on her forehead.

She came to the rear entrance, which she knew led into the kitchen. The screen door was closed, as was the door.

Carefully and slowly she pulled the screen door open. Thankfully, the well-oiled hinges made very little noise. Thank God for small blessings, she thought.

She turned the doorknob while holding the screen door open with the other hand. It wasn't locked. Her cheeks puffed out when she released the breath she'd been holding. There was a click as the lock disengaged.

She stopped and listened. Nothing. Gritting her teeth, she pushed the door in with the flat of her hand. Pausing, she listened again; still no sound from inside the little house.

Sticking her head inside the door, she peered into the dimly lit room. The blinds were shut and no lights were on. There wasn't a sound coming from inside except for the methodical ticking of the wall clock, hanging over the refrigerator.

The kitchen smelled of floor wax. The floor squeaked slightly as she stepped inside. She froze, holding her breath. No sound.

She made her way across the tiled kitchen floor to the archway on the far side of the room. Glancing around the corner, she looked down the small hallway to the living room. She could see a lump lying on the carpeted floor. It wasn't moving.

From somewhere outside, the sound of an engine started. The pickup truck. Damn.

Trudy hurried into the living room and pulled up blinds in time to see the blue pickup disappear up the road. Fuck. Alice was escaping.

She dropped the blinds and sat down heavily on the couch. Looking at the lump on the floor, she froze when she realized the shape was human. She dropped to her knees beside the body and rolled it on its back.

It was then she recognized the brunette she'd seen in the truck with Alice. Her throat had been slit ear to ear and her gray eyes stared unseeing up at Trudy. Blood still ran down the sides of her neck and pooled under her.

Trudy pictured Emily and her stomach heaved. Whoever did this had killed Emily in same the way. Maybe even with the same knife.

Trudy sighed. I'm too late again, she thought. But who is this woman? And why was she killed?

A sudden anger took hold of her. That bitch. Her mind raced with the sudden realization that Alice had killed Emily, not Miller—or Biggs, or whatever his name was. Alice killed Emily...

Now she was running. She'd get away unless someone stopped her. Trudy gritted her teeth. But Alice wasn't getting away not if Trudy Wilson had anything to say about it.

Twenty-Eight

ALICE WAS SATISFIED. She was about to make a clean get-away and there was no one to stop her. That stupid hairdresser and Sharon's moron brother couldn't stop her. And that bitch cop was in the hospital. Larry had been right about one thing; they were too stupid to figure out much of anything.

True, they had figured out who Sheriff Miller really was, but the hairdresser's fucking husband had conveniently rectified that problem.

She smirked. Pressing the gas pedal, she picked up speed. She'd be in LA in a day if she drove all night. Once she was on I-5, she'd be home free. In LA she'd shack up with friends and lay low until the heat lost her trail again.

No one knew what she'd done. No doubt there would be suspicions, but Larry had been a good teacher. He knew how cops thought and how to cover your tracks so you didn't leave any clues for the forensics guys.

Yup, I'm free and clear.

She rolled down the driver's window of the cab and the truck filled with salt air. She took a deep breath and smiled.

Resting her arm on the window frame, she felt the breeze flowing through her blonde hair.

The bloody clothes, gloves, and knife were in a burlap sack in the bed of the truck. She planned to stop at some rest stop on her way to California and dump the sack in a trash container. Then there wouldn't be anything to trace back to her.

The money Larry had been saving for them had been easy to get out of his widow. She was the last witness that could have ID'd her. She was dead now. Too bad.

Tracy Biggs, or should she say Glenda Miller, the nom de plume she'd used in Fairview, had been a nice person, but nice gals finished last—especially naive ones who married into the wrong family. She shrugged.

Five hundred gees of Fairview's money would go a long way toward building a new life in LA. One where she wouldn't have to turn tricks. Her life on her terms. No more pimps—no more drugs. Maybe she'd even meet one of those Beverly Hills millionaires and get married.

Glancing in the rearview mirror, she saw a small, red car speeding up behind her that looked all too familiar. She thought about pulling over to let it pass until she saw who was driving.

Bitch. The hairdresser. Fuck.

Alice gripped the steering wheel with both hands and stepped hard on the gas pedal. The truck quickly increased speed, causing the little car to lose ground. She smirked. I'll lose the bitch easy, she thought as she watched it recede in her mirror.

She rounded a curve on the highway. It had rows of trees blocking the view ahead, creating a blind corner.

She had to slow down when she almost ran into a large, slow-moving motor home. Shifting her foot to the brake pedal in time, she fought the truck as it fishtailed slightly before coming under control. The oncoming traffic made it impossible to pass on the two-lane highway. The smile faded from her lips. Her eyes flitted to the rearview mirror again. The hairdresser had closed the gap between them.

Alice frantically looked for a side street she might use as a bypass route to get ahead of the traffic. Behind her, the red car flashed its headlights. She wanted Alice to stop.

I'm not stopping for you or anyone else, bitch. No way.

Finally, a side street appeared about fifty yards ahead. Keeping her foot on the gas, she turned at the corner and gunned the engine. The truck swayed and fishtailed around the corner but managed to stay on four wheels. She pressed the gas pedal to the floor and the truck roared down the paved road until she was forced to screech to a stop at an intersection with a dead end sign on the road ahead.

The red car pulled up behind her. She decided to turn left. The road appeared to run parallel to the highway until it ended at a high cliff that ran beside the beach. Gunning the engine, she drove as fast as she could, occasionally glancing to her left between the houses. She caught intermittent glimpses of the highway. Now all she had to do was find another road to get there. She looked in the mirror and saw that Trudy had somehow managed to keep pace with her. Her brow wrinkled. I thought she said that car of hers was a piece of shit.

Unfortunately, she couldn't find a side street leading back to the highway. Alice got impatient. She stepped harder on the gas pedal, and the truck seemed to leap off the road beneath her. The needle on the speedometer said she was now up to eighty-five miles per hour.

The road ahead crested on a small rise and she was unable to see where it ended. She failed to notice a yellow, triangle-shaped sign in front of a three-slat wooden fence that marked the end of the road.

She smiled when she glanced in the mirror and saw she'd left the red car far behind. Goodbye, bitch. The wheels of the truck left the road as the truck crested the slight rise.

She froze when she realized she was out of road. Less than fifty feet away was a fence, beyond which was a short wall of rock and then the beach, and she was going way too fast to stop in time. Oh, shit!

She pressed both feet hard on the brake pedal and the truck slewed side-to-side, the tires screeching loudly. The truck shuddered around her, making her teeth rattle. She held on as the truck swerved again, then tipped over onto its side and slammed into the pavement with a crunch of metal accompanied by a shower of sparks.

Now on its side, the truck crashed through the fence and hit hard against the stonewall, shattering the windows. The momentum carried the wreckage over the wall and onto the beach beyond.

The heavy truck rolled four times until finally coming to rest on its roof. Parts of the truck were scattered behind it like breadcrumbs.

***

Trudy watched the truck rolling across the beach but managed to stop before she, too, ran off the road.

Putting the car in neutral, she flung open the driver's door. Racing across the sand, she got to the truck.

Kneeling down in the cold sand, she cupped her hands around her eyes and looked inside. No sign of Alice. She must've been thrown clear.

"Looking for me?"

Trudy turned slowly to see Alice, standing down the left side of the truck, holding a large hunting knife in her right hand.

Her hair was a tangled and her forehead had a long gash that was leaking blood in red trails down the left side of her face. Alice's eyes were hard and she was trembling, no doubt suffering from shock.

Trudy rose to her feet. She slipped out of her sandals. She might need the extra mobility in the wet sand.

Alice staggered toward her, the knife poised to strike. Her eyes were determined. "I'm gonna kill you, you fuckin' bitch."

Trudy backed up and held her hands up. "Now, Alice, there's no need for this. You're bleeding. You need help." Trudy continued to step backward. She thought she saw a flash of movement out of her left eye.

She stopped, but Alice continued to approach her. "Alice, come on now, put the knife down. It's over. Biggs is dead."

Alice still wasn't within striking distance when she stopped and swayed unsteadily. She glared at Trudy, her eyes filled with rage.

"You don't understand," Alice said, her voice breaking.

"Yes, I do. Biggs was using you like everyone used you, wasn't he?"

The blonde nodded. The knife began to lower slowly.

"You killed Emily didn't you?" asked Trudy. "And you called the police after you'd killed her didn't you?"

Alice nodded in response to both questions. As Trudy suspected the person who murdered Emily had to be the same person who called it in. It only made sense in a weird twisted logical sense.

"Why?"

"She couldn't have him and she knew too much. Biggs was mine and mine alone.

"I wasn't about to share what I got from him. The fuckin' bastard hated women; he used them, then, like garbage, threw them away. Like Sharon. Emily wanted a piece of my action, too." Alice slapped her chest with her left hand. "No fuckin' way."

"But why did you call it in?"

A wild-eyed Alice grinned making Trudy shiver inside. The woman was mad. "I wanted the cops to see what I'd done. They thought a mere woman couldn't kill with a knife." She scowled at Trudy. "But they were wrong! I did it. I slit her throat. Me. A mere woman." She spat the last few words spittle shooting from her mouth.

She again raised the knife. "And now you have to die." Alice staggered forward, the knife poised to kill.

"Stop right there." It was a man's voice.

Trudy turned in the direction of the voice. She froze when she saw Summers, standing with his pistol out and aiming at Alice. Where the hell had he come from?

His unsmiling face was focused on Alice. "Drop the knife," he said between gritted teeth.

Alice glared at him and her blue eyes narrowed. "You wouldn't hurt me, Kelly. Not after all the good times." She tried to appear seductive, but with the blood running down her left side, her hair askew, and a razor-sharp knife in her right hand, she didn't look particularly sexy at the moment.

Summers shook his head. "No, Alice, it's over." He moved closer, keeping his pistol aimed directly at Alice's midriff. "Drop the knife. I won't say it again."

He pulled the hammer back on his pistol. Trudy heard it lock into place.

Alice, her face twisted in anger, started toward him, the knife now held up over her head. He stood his ground.

Trudy watched them move steadily closer to each other, knowing how this would end.

Just as Alice was about to slash the knife downward into him, Summers fired. Alice's eyes grew wide and a trail of blood came from the side of her mouth when she coughed. The knife fell from her grasp to land in the gray sand. Her blue eyes lost their inner light. She gasped and collapsed onto her side then lay still her eyes focused only on infinity.

Trudy rushed to kneel next to her. Summers stood staring at them with the gun still pointed at Alice.

Trudy put one arm underneath the dying young woman's head. "Alice," she said.

Alice's eyes focused on Trudy. Her eyes were filled with tears. "I had no idea it would hurt so much," she said. Her body stiffened briefly, then relaxed as the last of her strength disappeared. Her eyes gazed, unseeing, at the cloudless, blue-sky overhead.

Trudy gently laid her head in the sand, then stood up next to the dead woman.

"Well, that's it then, isn't it, Deputy?"

He nodded and lowered his weapon to his side, then let it drop from his fingertips onto the sand.

"Freeze where you are and raise your hands above your heads."

Trudy turned her head slightly to look up the beach toward the sound of the voice. Three state troopers, brandishing their automatics, were running down the beach toward them. Trudy and Summers raised their arms over their heads as the troopers encircled them.

A trooper, his blond hair cut military-style, spoke first. "What's going on here?" His voice was gruff and deep, his steely gaze watched them warily.

"You got a spare month?" asked Trudy, her face impassive.

The trooper frowned, kept his gun leveled at them, then signaled to the other two troopers to cuff them. As one approached, he kicked Summers pistol away, then holstered his weapon and grabbed Summers' right wrist, folding his arm behind him. He completed cuffing him as his partner did the same to Trudy.

"We received a call from A neighbor lady saying you needed immedaite assistance. Since you hekpedc one of our own we came running." The trooper grinned. Trudy knew he meant Detective Sanchez. "We broke a few speed limits but we obviously showed up in time."

Trudy grinned her knees trembling.

"But we have a lot of unanswered questions," said the blond trooper, holstering his pistol.

"So do I," said Trudy, who gazed unblinkingly into his brown eyes. "So do I."

The troopers led her and ther handcuffed Summers up the gray beach toward two police cruisers, the lights on the roof of the cars flashing red and blue, parked next to her red Chevette. The POS was still running. A trail of exhaust drifted lazily from the tailpipe of her car like some ghostly apparition. She smiled to herself as a sense of relief washed over her. *Good ol' gal.*

Epilogue

THREE DAYS AFTER THE EVENTS ON THE BEACH, Bruce was released from the hospital. Trudy met him in the waiting area. A raven-haired nurse's aide pushed him in a wheelchair. He appeared embarrassed at having to ride. Hospital rules, the nurse told him when he signed the release papers.

Trudy ran up and wrapped her arms around him, making his face flush crimson.

"Trudy, it's okay. I'm fine," he said.

She stepped back and stood beaming at him with her arms crossed. "I'm so glad you're all right."

Bruce used both hands to push himself out the wheelchair. He wobbled for a moment, then, once his equilibrium returned, he walked toward the door. His habitual bouncy pace was slower than usual, not surprising given the injury to his leg.

Trudy walked with him to the parking lot. She beamed at him. He smiled thinly.

"When's Sanchez gettin' out?" asked Bruce.

"She was transferred to Portland General last night. I'm told they have a pretty good Physical Therapy department there."

Bruce nodded.

As the doors slid aside, the breeze struck them. It carried the smells of the flowers blooming in the hospital garden that lined the walkways toward the parking lot.

They soon arrived at Trudy's little red Chevette. "Still a piece of shit?" asked Bruce, his pale, hazel eyes dancing.

"No. In fact, the opposite."

Bruce grinned and Trudy laughed as she opened her door and got in. She reached across and pulled up the button to unlock the passenger door. Bruce got in without hitting his head.

"You're getting pretty good at that," Trudy said.

Bruce chuckled in response.

Trudy started the car, then drove out the exit and onto the highway.

"Where we goin'?" asked Bruce.

"I asked Rocky to drive you back to Seattle. You know, since your bike is fucked."

"You two...?"

She shrugged. "I don't know, exactly. We'll see."

He nodded. "Did Sanchez ever tell you why she suspected Alice?"

Trudy laughed. "That bothered you, too, huh? Yeah, I asked her. She told me she didn't know for sure, but when Alice knew about the body up the street, it occurred to her she was involved. She just didn't know how."

Bruce nodded. "The little bitch sure had us fooled, didn't she?"

Trudy glanced at him. "Yeah. For sure. Well, think about it, we had zero chance of solving this thing. We're not trained detectives. How many times do you think we should've died? Talk about a dumbass idea, thinking we could solve Sharon's murder. You and I are the king and queen of dumbasses."

Bruce chuckled. "For sure."

Trudy changed the subject. "Sanchez said there were photos all over Miller's office wall of him with the Portland PD, and all of them were Photoshop fakes."

Bruce grunted. "Figures. Bastard got what he deserved." Bruce's brow wrinkled. "The lady living near Sharon's place called the state cops?" She nodded.

"Why did they react so fast?"

"They said because we helped Sanchez. And I suspect they had the sheriff and his deputy under surveillance for a while. Why else would Sanchez be ion town when the murders happened? Coincidence? I don't think so." She shook her head. "If Sanchez thinks we buy that shit she's dealing with the wrong fuckin' people."

Bruce grinned his expression one of relief reflecting how she felt.

Trudy sat in silence, staring at the road ahead, following the coast highway to her turnoff. She turned at Bard Street and started the familiar trip between the rows of swaying pines. A gentle breeze had sprung up. The sky was overcast, but it wasn't raining. Not a bad day.

They went down the hill to park in front of her neat, split-level house. Her home. Her refuge. She turned off the engine, then shifted in her seat to face him.

"We did what we had to do, you know," Trudy said. "Don't you believe that?"

Bruce shrugged and grinned. "Yeah. Sure."

Trudy was confident they'd done the right thing. Two deadly murderers had been brought to justice. That had to count for something. Bruce would see it when he had time to digest all that had happened.

They got out of the car and walked toward the front door of her house. They were a team. A team that had faced a case of shear murder and solved it.

About the Author

International selling author, Russ Crossley, writes science fiction and fantasy, and mystery/suspense.

The second book in his science fiction satire series, Revenge of the Lushites, released by 53rd Street Publishing in the fall of 2013, is available now in e-book and trade paperback.

Several of his short stories have appeared in anthologies from 53rd Street Publishing, WMG Publishing, Pocket Books, and St. Martins Press. His short story, available now at Over My Dead Body online Mystery magazine, is titled Instrument of Justice.

Contact him on Facebook, Twitter, or his website www. russcrossley.com.

Other books by the Author

Razor and Edge Mysteries
The Kidnapping of Billy Buttons
String of Pearls
Death by Clown
Beggin' For Murder
Ragged Ice
The Grand Central Mystery
A Strange Case of Undead Murder

Jazz Stiletto Mysteries
A Day Without Sunshine
Skullduggery
Instrument of justice (first published in Over My Dead Body online
mystery magazine)

The Amanda Dark paranormal mysteries
Hook Island
Grind Manor
Moonrise Diner

The Trudy Wilson Mysteries
Bad Loyalty
Shear Murder
Buzzcut coming in 2015

Novels
Attack of the Lushites
Revenge of the Lushites
My Zombie Prince
Antique Virgin
The Fire In Their Hearts
with R.S. Meger (from Champagne Books)
Zomopolis
The Last Serial Killer

Short Stories
Countdown
Shoeless Moe
Round Up At The Burger Bar:
The Story of Trixie Pug, Parts 1, 2, 3, 4, 5, 6, 7, 8, 9
Five Minutes
Blossom Queen, Barbarian
The Secret
The Family Line
End of the Flies
Death by Magic
The Penguin Sleeps With The Fishes
Only The Worthy
Hero For A Day
End of Empire
Strange Bedfellows
Big Business
A Perfect Crime
The Wise Guy and The Pirates
In Search of the Perfect Cup
T.I.N. Men
The Legend of G and the Dragonettes
The Incredible Mr. Fix-It
Lock Stock and Barrel
Divided Loyalties
Cave of Wonders
A Family Empire
Until We Meet Again
Dragon Rising
Solitary Man
The Keel Mountain Conspiracy
Angel on My Shoulder
Heroes of Old
The Great Bicycle Race
Tikka's Big Day
"My Partner the Zombie" —
Hungry For Your Love Anthology

(St. Martin's Press)
Big Hairy Deal
One Red Shoe
A Bad Day in Lunden Texas
Bloody Betty, Queen of the Pirates
Mirror Image
Dangerous Waters
Cape Disappointment
Boomerang
The Watcher of Wayburn Street
The Apprentice
Drip!
A Beautiful Friendship and The Parrot of Doom
Robine's Diary
The Christmas Club
Loose Ends
Splatter Pattern
It Takes Two
Lexicon

Anthologies
Tales of Urban Fantasy
Five Tales of Bizarre Detectives
Tales of Mystery and Suspense
Tales of Weird Fantasy
Spies, Detectives, & Heroes
Tales of Twisted Crime
Tales of The Unexpected
Tales From Space
10 by Russ Crossley
Round Up At The Burger Bar: The Story of Trixie Pug,
Parts 1- 5 The Beginning
Worlds of Science Fiction and Fantasy
More Tales of Mystery and Suspense
Ladies of the Jolly Roger
Justice Served
Love Stories

Ladies of the Jolly Roger with R.S. Meger
The Adventures of Razor and Edge:
Five Tales From The Quirky Detective Team

Non-Fiction
The Writers Tools - The Synopsis

On the following pages is a sample of the thriller, The Last Serial Killer, available to order in trade paperback from your favorite book store or as an eBook from your favorite online retailer.

In the not-too-distant future, medical advances rid the world of serial killers forever—all except one: The Last Serial Killer.

That killer is about to wreak havoc. Using right-wing radio host and Gulf War III veteran Todd Road as an unwilling conduit to aliens who claim he's innocent, the killer gets out of prison.

Todd and FBI agent Angela Cody join forces to recapture the killer—encountering a bloody trail of bodies, a future America thrown into chaos by fear and confusion, and deadly marauders bent on murder—and follow clues to a final, twisted, horrifying end.

A story of suspense, blending murder and justice with a dash of science fiction unlike anything you've ever read.

"A futuristic, suspenseful page-turner about a killer who enjoys his grisly work." — R.S. Meger, Author of The *Scarlet Curse*.

ONE

"They're coming." The caller's voice in his earpiece was barely above a whisper.

Todd Road's gray eyes scanned the list of names and link numbers on the white computer screen recessed into his work station. The glossy black desk, extended from the control board console, was covered in touch-screen buttons and indicators for sound and light levels in KZAP's studio. His heart beat faster when his eyes locked on the caller's name and the origin of the call.

Todd drew in a breath and held it, his chest tightening. It was him. Serial murderer Mike Sikes was calling his show again. And Elmore Watts said radio was dead back in '22? What the hell did he know. In 2067, talk radio was once again the king of all media. (At least, according to Smith & Wesson, his principal sponsor.)

Guy Thompson, the KZAP news director and his boss, was pressuring Todd to get rid of this nut. But nuts were the staple of his show, and Sikes was the craziest and highest-rated nut every listener loved to hate. The ad revenues for the station had tripled in the last six moths since Sikes started calling. But Guy, like many a new bride, was getting cold feet. Depending on a serial murderer for ratings wasn't his idea of good radio.

The more Mike called, the more Todd found himself agreeing with Guy. He'd made a vow to himself to only take three more calls, then he'd cut the bastard loose.

"What do you mean, Mike?" he asked unenthusiastically.

"The aliens are coming. To Earth. They want to know why."

Mike Sikes's voice was surprisingly calm for someone who had just edged over the crazy line. Sikes had finally lost touch with reality, as if he'd ever been in this reality with everyone else.

Not that Todd knew how crazy was supposed to sound. Many of the callers to his program—On the Road with Todd Road, The Conservative's Conservative—were on the fringe of mainstream society, but he wouldn't call them crazy. Exactly. They were patriots. Honest, hard-working Americans, average folks let down by their government. A view he shared.

"Mike, you know my opinions on little green men from other planets."

"I know, Mr. Road, but they've been speaking to me for a long time, and they need my help. That's why they're coming here."

He sounded serious. Todd thought it was time to give the guy a blast, something he'd perfected in his ten years behind the microphone, and get rid of this loony.

"Sure, Mike, there are aliens inside your head talking to you. Just you, no one else in the world, just good ol' boy Mike Sikes, serial killer. Sure, that sounds plausible." Todd made a circle by the side of his head, which made his producer, on the other side of the glass wall, grin and chuckle.

Amy Rickland, a flaxen-haired woman of thirty-five, was a damn good producer—a fact Todd frequently told the station manager—and she was a staunch conservative, which made her a real find in the world of talk radio. Being slim and attractive didn't hurt, either.

"You can make fun of me all you want," said Mike, sounding not the least bit upset at Todd's attempt to humiliate him on national radio. "But I'm telling you, they'll be here in a week's time, and they'll be looking for you."

Todd's gray-streaked eyebrows rose in surprise. "Me? Mike, why would they want to meet a little ol' radio guy like me?"

He winked at Amy, who smiled. She signaled they had to break for the news in thirty seconds.

"You're the only one who knows I'm innocent."

Anger flared in Todd. He'd being saying this to stir up his audience. He never expected Mike to believe he actually supported the sonofabitch bloody killer. "Well, folks, that's about all we need to hear from Massacre Mike." He hit the cutoff button, ending the call. "Time for the news at the top of the hour. We'll be back in ten."

The red, on-air light over the glass wall went dark. He stole a glance at the digital clock on the control board. He had ten minutes, and his bladder was screaming for relief.

Todd pulled the ear-mike from his right ear, then rose stiffly from his maroon-colored chair. He stretched his arms over his head, his ample belly straining against the white plastic buttons that ran down his light indigo shirt.

I'm getting old, thought Todd. He ran one bloated hand over his hairless head.

Amy opened the door to the booth. "Hey, boss, you think that guy knows something we don't?"

Todd glanced at her and smiled sardonically, "Never believe everything you hear. Especially in the talk-radio business, my sweet."

Striding through the open door, he passed a chuckling Amy and was soon standing over a urinal in the men's room. Too much coffee again this morning. When was he going to learn?

Maybe Mike was telling the truth, at least as he knew it. Todd didn't think murderers were crazy—psychotic, sure, but they deserved to reap what they sowed. Death was too good from them. Mike may be a loon, but he sure sounded convinced he'd been talking to real aliens. So if Mike wasn't making any of this up, why include Todd?

Todd zipped his fly, reminding himself that he wanted no part of Mike Sikes or his kooky ideas. But since had had helped Mike create the fantasy of his innocence to pump up his ratings, he did feel a certain obligation to let the madness roll on until they stuck the needle in Mike's arm.

"Then it's good riddance to the stinking garbage," he muttered to himself. He glanced in the mirror. "Some days, Road, I don't like you very much," he said to his reflection.

As he washed his hands, he made up his mind to tell Amy to ban the guy from the show. Guy was right, Mike had been calling long enough. Since Mike was the last of his kind (medical science had seen to that), he'd managed to squeeze a few perks out of the warden.

Two years on death row must have bent the guy's brain severely out of shape. Didn't matter, anyway; another six months and he was going to fry. Well, not exactly fry. It would be more like death by drug overdose, which had been the preferred method of execution for the Department of Corrections for several decades.

Todd pitied Mike's victims far more than their murderer. They had suffered painful, lingering deaths at his hands. Mike wouldn't suffer, but at least he'd be dead. As far as Todd was concerned, the system was too lenient with these guys. Maybe he'd discuss that in the next segment.

The heartless monster had inspired whole new discussions around the death penalty, one of Todd's favorite topics. He had hoped to have Mike on the show one more time, just before he was sent to the great beyond. But now Mike was trying to change his carefully crafted agenda and talk about little green men. Todd had already spoken with the program director about scheduling the event, his code name for Mike's execution. He smiled at himself in the mirror over the sink. "You're sooo smart, Mr. Road," he said to his reflection.

The smile faded as he gazed at the dark circles under his gray eyes.

"But you look like shit, Road. You gotta get some sleep one of these nights," he murmured. Insomnia was a curse in his family.

He sighed and left the men's room, heading back to the booth. Amy greeted him at the door with a stunned look on her face. Her heavy layer of makeup couldn't hide the pallor of her skin and the fear in her eyes.

"What's wrong?" he asked.

"Guy... from the newsroom called up..." Her voice trailed off to an unintelligible whisper.

Her body trembled.

"What?" Was it a death in her family, was it in his family? Not that he had much of one left. At forty, he wasn't married, though he did have a sister, Izzy, who lived in Baltimore with her husband and two kids. He tried to recall Izzy's husband's name, but it eluded him.

Amy looked at him with watery eyes. She was always so controlled and calm about things that seeing her like this shook him to the core.

Placing his meaty hands on her narrow shoulders, her held her. She was really trembling, almost as if she'd been in a walk-in freezer like the ones they had in restaurants, and couldn't get her temperature back up.

"They're here," she whispered finally from between trembling lips.

"Who's here?" he asked. His guts were twisted by fear, struggling to comprehend what he already suspected

The aliens had arrived.

She shook her head. "Mike was right...."

Todd let go of her shoulders and hurried into the newsroom. His show was over for the moment.

Heads turned as he walked in. Guy sat in his office, barking orders to his staff from behind his desk. He was frantically typing an e-mail, his fingers pounding the keyboard, when Todd entered the noisy room.

The office reeked of stale coffee and donuts, a reporter's primary food groups. The reporters around the room wore ear-links and gazed at their computer screens, mesmerized by something they were seeing.

Todd walked to the nearest workstation, where a reporter he knew only as Mary sat transfixed, staring at the image on her screen.

Todd moved closer to look over her shoulder. His heart rate increased at the sight of a shot obviously from the Hubble V telescope. The object in the center of the screen was a vessel—a space ship, a flying saucer—whatever he called it, it was what every sci-fi fan would instantly recognize as an alien spacecraft.

The ship was long and shaped like a cigar. There wasn't a fiery tail, like in those cheap sci-fi flicks of so long ago, but the object moved across the screen as he watched. At the bottom right of the screen was the word 'LIVE' with the red letters of the CNN logo beside it.

"This is real," he whispered. Mary nodded, her arms crossed over her red blouse, her blonde hair golden in the glare of the overhead florescent lights.

Todd broke away and rushed into Guy's office, slamming the door behind him. The glass in the wood-framed door rattled as it closed.

Guy glared at him. He was completely bald; a few years previously he'd begun to shave the fringe that was all that remained of his once-brown hair. His intense blue eyes were fixed on Todd.

He sat behind a glass-topped desk in a high-backed, brown leather executive chair. On the wall behind him were numerous—too many to count—certificates and holographs of him with some of the country's leading movers and shakers in the radio, political, and movie industries. In all of the pictures, Guy wore a wide, toothpaste smile.

Right now, though, Guy looked none too happy.

"Did you know about this?" he asked in his gravely voice.

To Todd, his boss's voice had always sounded like an old-fashioned washboard. At least it reminded him of the one in the virtual display in the museum on Central Street.

Todd threw his hands up, his frustration about to boil over. "For God's sake, Guy, the man's a loony. He's said a lot of things on my show. You know what psychos are like. You can't believe half of what they say. You know that."

Guy ground his teeth, a habit that made Todd wince. Todd thought he smelled smoke, even though smoking of any kind hadn't been allowed in office buildings for the past fifty years. "The biggest story in human history, and we coulda had an exclusive."

This pile-on of revelations had taken a toll on Todd's senses—his knees were trembling from too much input, and he sank down onto one of the two steel-framed chairs in front of Guys expansive desk before he collapsed. "Guy. It's not my fault. I mean, how was I supposed to know aliens were real? How would anyone know something like that?"

Guy flipped around his flat computer monitor so Todd could see the space ship, gaining ground as it raced toward Earth from the depths of space. The reflective, mirror-like surface of the craft stood out against the black of space. An eerie glow surrounded the surface of the ship.

According to the caption, scientists from the Jet Propulsion Laboratory in Pasadena said the alien craft was on a trajectory toward Earth from somewhere outside the solar system. According to telemetry data, just before the alien craft entered the solar system, it reduced velocity from just under the speed of light to a reasonably slower 20,000 KPS, and had been slowing ever since.

Todd shook his head, trying to clear this impossible scene from his mind. No, he wasn't dreaming. This was definitely for real; it was happening.

"Get Sikes on the line, and this time I want a straight interview. None of that humiliation crap you're so good at," said Guy, with a thread of deep sarcasm running through his thick voice.

Todd nodded as he watched the screen, transfixed by the events unfolding before his eyes. This was ridiculous. Until now, he'd believed in aliens about as much as he believed in Santa Claus. This was going to bring out all the crazies. His show would become a circus. Great for ratings, but he wondered what the longer-term ramifications were going to be.